Middle School Is Worse Than Meatloaf

Also by Jennifer L. Holm

Babymouse series (with Matthew Holm)
Boston Jane: *Wilderness Days*
Boston Jane: *An Adventure*
Boston Jane: *The Claim*
The Creek
Our Only May Amelia
The Trouble with May Amelia
Penny from Heaven
Stink Files series (with Jonathan Hamel)
Turtle in Paradise

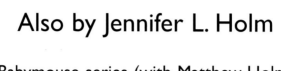

Middle School Is Worse Than Meatloaf

A YEAR TOLD THROUGH STUFF

Ginny

YOUR NAME HERE

atheneum books for young readers
new york london toronto sydney

by Jennifer L. Holm

pictures by Elicia Castaldi

For Ralph Slotten, my favorite poet
—J. L. H.

To dad, my two favorite Judys, and
to David—with hearts
—E. C.

Many thanks to Ginee Seo! You rock!
—J. L. H. and E. C.

Drawings for "The Adventures of Henry
and Ginny" by Matthew Holm

Ginny's Back-to-School Shopping List

1. new school shoes and new toe shoes for ballet.

2. new backpack

3. new binder (a COOL one this year. P<u>lease</u>!! Brown is <u>not</u> a cool color!!!)

4. the yellow sweater at the mall. The one in the window of Gerard's.

$68.00

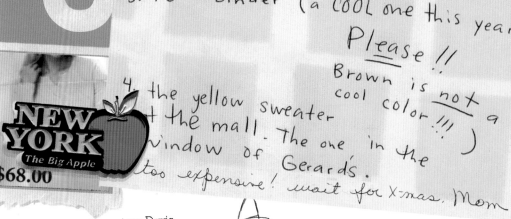

shoes for ballet.
2. new backpack *your toe shoes are just fine*

3. new binder (a COOL one this year.
Please!!
Brown is not a
cool color!!!)

4. the yellow sweater *at the mall. The one in the window of Gerards. too expensive! wait for X-mas. Mom*

Student: Genevieve Davis

Grade: 7

Homeroom: Angelini, Rm. #212

Period	Subject	Rm.	Teacher	Days
1	Phys. Ed.	Gym	Simkins	M/W/F
1	Health Education	Gym	Simkins	T/Th
2	Life Science	212	Angelini	*
3	Social Studies	112	Poehlman	*
4	Art	121	Willis	*
5	Mathematics	201	DiGiuseppi	*
Lunch (12:14 - 12:42) YES!				
6	English	113	Cusumano	*
7	Club	TBD	TBD	M/W/F
7	Library	Lib.	Zamaillian	T/Th
8	Study Hall	102	Franklin	*

* = Class meets daily
TBD = To Be Determined

Bus: #20

School starts promptly at 8:15.

Permission slips required for all after-school activities

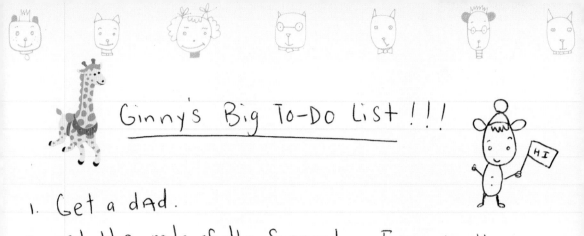

Ginny's Big To-Do List!!!

1. Get a dad.
2. get the role of the Sugarplum Fairy in the Nutcracker.
3. Look good in the school photo for once.!!!!
4. Do something with hair to make nose look smaller. Color?? Perm??

5. Win something. Anything.
6. Try to be friends with Mary Catherine Kelly.
7. Get pink sweater back!!
8. Convince mom to let me go see Grampa Joe over Easter break.
9. Get Henry to chill out.
10. Ignore horoscopes whenever possible.

WOODLAND BANK
"Your Hometown Bank"

ACCOUNT NO.	ACCOUNT TYPE		STATEMENT PERIOD
4357287	WORRY - FREE CHECKING		Aug. 1 - Sept. 1

Genevieve Davis
Melinda Davis (guardian)
2610 Lark Lane
Woodland Glen, PA 18762
llllllllllllllllllllllllllll

Posting Date	Transaction Description	Deposits & Interests	Checks & Subtractions	Daily Balance
				$5.00
				$30.00
	BEGINNING BALANCE			$5.00
08-01	DEPOSIT	+ $25.00	– $25.00	$10.00
08-04	ATM	+ $5.00		$5.00
08-07	DEPOSIT		– $5.00	$25.00
08-11	ATM	+ $20.00		$5.00
08-14	DEPOSIT		– $20.00	$20.00
08-18	ATM	+ $15.00		$5.00
08-18	DEPOSIT		– $15.00	$5.00
08-25	ATM			$5.00
08-27				
08-31	ENDING BALANCE			

Chamomile Calming Tea

Mom--

Reasons <u>It Is Good</u> to Buy the Sweater

1. It will warm my arms and make me finish my homework faster.
2. It will make my nose look smaller.
3. It will make me so happy I will babysit Timmy on friday night (for free!)
4. Everyone needs a sweater. Winter is coming.
5. It will keep me from catching a cold and missing school.
6. You can always borrow it if you want.

your sweaterless daughter,
Ginny

PISCES

Get ready, Pisces! The fall has always been a time of excitement for you, and this year is no diferent. Change is in the air!

Lucky Numbers: 4, 15, 18, 21

TUESDAY, September 5

I wish you'd clean
your room my mom says.
But I cleaned it
last month, I say,
what difference does it make?
Will it stop world hunger?
Will it make the rain forest
stop disappearing?
Will it cure cancer?
No, but I might
consider buying
the sweater
if you do.

golfer's paradise
Fairway Heaven

FOR my FAVORITE
GRANDDAUGHTER,
HAVE A GREAT FIRST
DAY OF SEVENTH GRADE!

LOVE,
GRAMPA JOE
(A.K.A. THE OLD GUY IN
FLORIDA!)

There's nothing quite like
the first day of school.
with all those
newly waxed floors
and hopeful faces.
You can't help but think
you'll get a fresh start
and be the girl
everyone thinks is cool,
not the one who got whacked
by a softball in gym
and had her nose
swell to the size of the
Empire State Building.
There's nothing quite like
the first day of school,
you think,
and then Brian Bukvic
shouts,
"Hey, Banana Nose!"
and you know you're
back in school.

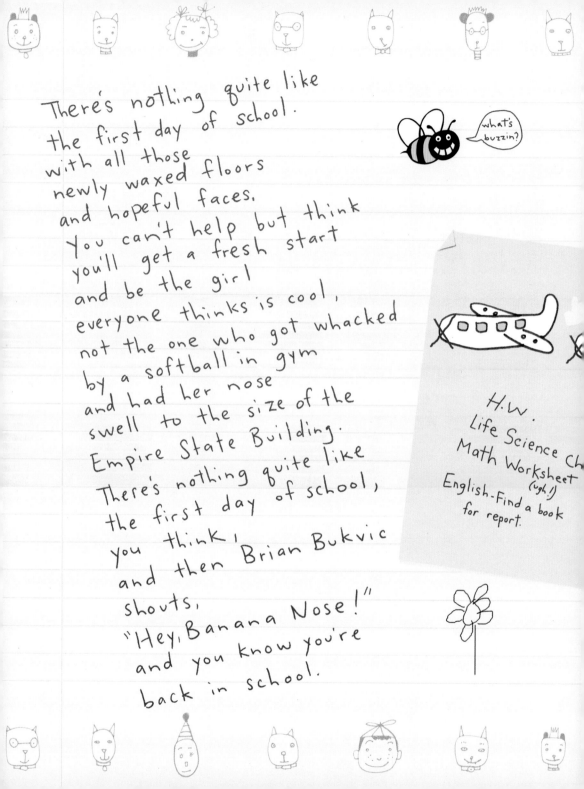

what's
buzzin?

H.W.
Life Science Ch
Math Worksheet
(ugh!)
English-Find a book
for report.

Heartbreakerz Lip Shine

Budget :
allowance (weekly) $5.00
babysitting (1 night) $20.00

People to hit up for babysitting so that I can buy the sweater.

1. Generos - Susie (2) + Mary (3)
   Little kids. In bed by 8. Cool dud player
   and every movie ever made.

2. Bakers - Ben (baby) Good sleeper.
          Diapers are gross.

3. Williams - Larry (7) + Marvin (5) + Bobby (3)
   Good snacks.

4. Brendshaw - Ollie (4)
   Pretty good. Except for the watching Barney part

5. Mullens - Shawn (9)
Great video games !! Fun kid even though he always wins.

6. Kurtz - Tiffany (1) ?????
   Total brat. Sara Patel says Tiffany bit her.

PRIVATE PHYSICIAN'S REPORT OF
PHYSICAL EXAMINATION OF A PUPIL OF SCHOOL AGE

LAST NAME: Davis
FIRST NAME: Genevieve (Ginny)
NAME OF SCHOOL: Woodland Central
GRADE: 7
HOMEROOM: Angelini, rm# 212
ADDRESS: 2610 Lark Lane, Woodland Glen, PA 18762
AGE: 12
SEX: Female
BIRTH DATE: February 23

SIGNIFICANT MEDICAL CONDITIONS   (PLEASE CHECK)

	YES	NO	If yes, explain
ALLERGIES	X Milk;		Allergy shots as needed
ASTHMA		X	
CARDIAC		X	
DIABETES		X	
HEARING DISORDER		X	
RESPIRATORY ILLNESS		X	
SEIZURE		X	
OTHER		X	

REPORT OF PHYSICAL EXAMINATION

HEIGHT (inches)	59
WEIGHT (lbs)	89
PULSE	80
BP	100/70
EYES COLOR	brown
VISION	20/20
EARS R / L	normal / normal
HAIR/SCALP	blonde / normal
NOSE/THROAT	normal
TEETH/GINGIVA	normal
LYMPH/GLANDS	normal
HEART	normal
LUNGS	normal
ABDOMEN	normal
EXTREMITIES	normal
SPINE	normal
NEUROMUSCULAR	normal
IMMUNIZATIONS	up-to-date, see attached

COMMENTS: *Patient presents as a healthy 12 year old. Height and weight on 95th percentile growth curve*

Dr. Butler

Signature of Physician

Madame Cecile's
Ballet Academy

Announcement

Tryouts for the winter recital of the
Nutcracker ballet
to be held November 6
promptly at 4:00 P.M.

My teacher Miss Angelini
told us to describe ourselves in ten words.
My
Name
Is
Ginny
And
I
Am
A
Girl.
Whew, that wasn't hard,
it pretty much says it all.
I just hope the period
counts as a word.

Ginny

Becky

Hi Ginny,
I'm so happy we're in homeroom together!
Miss Angelini is really cool. My sister had her
last year.
Becky Soo
W/B (write back)

P.S. Want to sit together at lunch? ♡

Hi Becky Soo,
Miss Angelini seems pretty nice
although she gave me a funny look
when I said that I was Henry
Davis's sister.
Mom and Bob have another date on
Friday!! Yay!! I just know that he's
going to ask mom to marry him,
as long as my stupid brother doesn't
scare him off first. Timmy threw
up on the front seat of Bob's car.

Ginny   P.S. I can't wait for lunch.
W/B   P.P.S. Except if it's meatloaf day.
             P.P.P.S. do you think middle school
                   is worse than meatloaf?

Hi Ginny,
Wow! I've never even been on a date
(except if you count
Jack Gillian kissing me in kindergarden,
which I don't)
Becky Soo!
W/B
P.S. I'm pretty sure it's meatloaf day!
     I sure hope not!

Ginny Davis, Period 6

Teacher: Mr. Cusumano

English Assignment: Compose Three Haikus

Perfect!

A+
very unusual
subject but
well done!
mr. C

Three Meatloaf Haikus

Oh yucky meatloaf
sitting under the hot lights
so gray and gristly.

Nothing tastes worse than
you, not cauliflower or
even lima beans.

And what is that weird
thing sticking out--a whisker?
hair? a rubber band?

Dear Parents,

Seventh graders will be having their annual school photos taken on Thursday, September 21st. Please have your child dress accordingly.

Proofs will be available one month after photos have been taken.

Sincerely,
Mrs. MacGillicuty
Principal

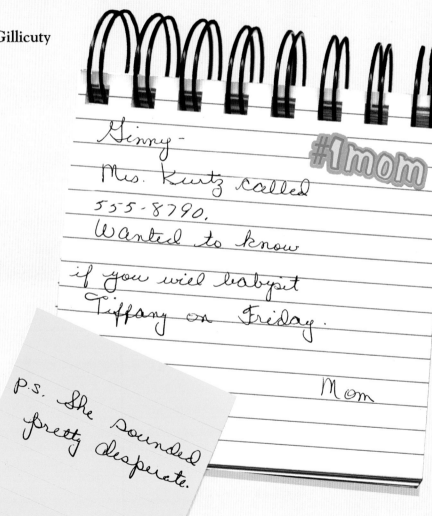

Ginny —

Mrs. Kurtz called 555-8790. Wanted to know if you will babysit Tiffany on Friday.

Mom

P.S. She sounded pretty desperate.

Salon
1915 Ideal Drive
Woodland Glen, PA 18762

September 21

Client: Ginny Davis

Hair color treatment (color reversal from red to blonde) $100.00

Haircut and style (to remove burned ends) $ 35.00

Subtotal $135.00

Tax $ 8.10

TOTAL $143.10

Melinda Davis
2610 Lark Lane
Woodland Glen, PA 18762

2612

Pay to the
order of _____

Date_____

$ _____

WOODLAND BANK   "your hometown bank"

Dollars _____

For_____

|:0 1

DAY TELEPHONE
555-1508

NIGHT TELEPHONE
AFTER 6:00 P.M.
555-8488

VITO'S PLUMBING
VITO MONTECALVO, MASTER PLUMBER #2842
PLUMBING AND HEATING
GAS   OIL BURNERS   VENTILATION

TERMS: 30 DAYS NET

A SERVICE CHARGE OF 2%
PER MONTH WILL APPLY ON
ALL OVER 30 DAY ACCOUNTS

Date	Description		Amount
9-19	emergency call after 6:00 p.m.		$75.00
	replacement parts damaged		
	by bubble bath in jacuzzi jets		$200.00
	labor		$175.00
	subtotal		$450.00
	tax		$27.00
	total		$477.00

ACCOUNT DUE AND PAYABLE UPON RECEIPT OF STATEMENT. A MINIMUM $2.00
REBILLING CHARGE WILL BE ADDED TO ALL ACCOUNTS 30 DAYS PAST DUE.

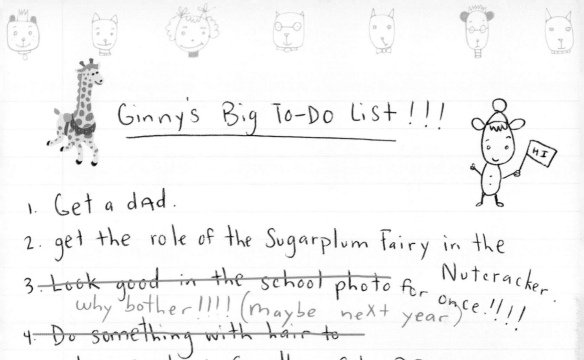

Ginny's Big To-Do List!!!

1. Get a dad.
2. get the role of the Sugarplum Fairy in the Nutcracker.
3. ~~Look good in the school photo for once.!!!!~~ *why bother!!!! (maybe next year)*
4. ~~Do something with hair to make nose look smaller. Color?? Perm??~~ *Leave alone until it grows back!!!!!!!!!*
5. Win something. Anything.
6. Try to be friends with Mary Catherine Kelly.
7. Get pink sweater back!!
8. Convince mom to let me go see Grampa Joe over Easter break.
9. Get Henry to chill out.
10. Ignore horoscopes whenever possible.

Ginny Davis, Period 6

Teacher: Mr. Cusumano

English Assignment: Describe Something You Lost

Please be descriptive. 150-word minimum.

A+
excellent!
M. C

My Dad

My dad went out for some milk when I was a little kid and never came home.

See, this seventeen-year-old boy called Tony Ramone who lived on the other side of town thought it was a good idea to drink a bunch of beer and then go driving. There was my dad sitting at the corner of Pine and Oak and Tony Ramone came speeding up in his big truck and slammed right into my dad and he was killed just like that.

Tony was fine, and you would think that killing somebody would make him straighten up but after that he got into two more accidents and finally drove his truck into the side of the O'Hara's house in the middle of the night.

Thanks to stupid Tony Ramone I can't drink milk anymore without breaking out in hives, and I used to like cereal a lot, especially the sugar kind.

Not to mention I **really** miss my dad.

(162 words)

Knock knock.
Who's there?
Hair.
Hair who?
Hair today, gone tomorrow!

My mom cut off her hair.
It's short and
she looks young,
like a movie star.
New man, new hair,
she laughs,
getting ready
for her date.

She has had
long black hair
my whole life
and now it's gone.
Your father loved
my long
hair, she says.
I want to say
I did too.

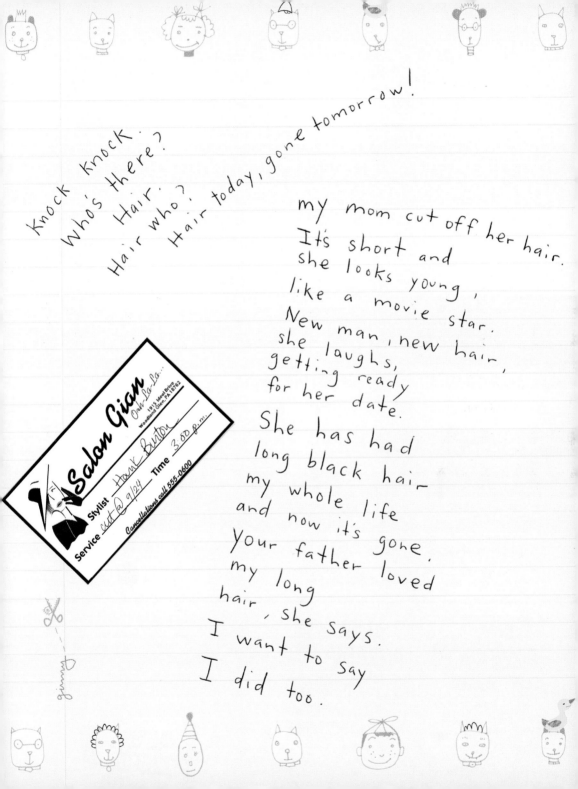

Salon Gian
Ooh-La-La
1913 Ideal Drive
Woodland Glen, PA 18762

Stylist _Hank Burton_
Service _Cut @ 9/24_ Time _3:00 p.m._

Cancellations call 555-0600

Ginny

1. Bob and I will be having dinner at
                Mario's # 555-2100.

2. Order a pizza from Al's for dinner.

3. If you let Hoover out, remember to
      let him back in. Same goes for Fluffy.

4. Don't stay up too late.

     Love,
       Mom

P.S. Do Not let your little brother eat the
toothpaste like he did last time. It is
not food for him. And we are running
out of toothpaste.

THE ADVENTURES OF HENRY & GINNY

...TO HAVE FUN!

BY H. Davis

It's no secret that
the police knew
our house by heart ♡
and the neighbors
sometimes look
worriedly
at their mailboxes
when he walks by.
And I know he has
a bad habit of
lighting fireworks
in the teachers' lounge
and breaking into other
kids' lockers.
But the thing is,
he's always been
the one to stick up for me
and make me laugh,
and doesn't that count
for something?
Besides he's the only person
I know who can suck milk
through a straw up his nose.
Henry may be a juvenile delinquent,
but he's still my favorite brother.

TEACHER

Dear Mrs. Davis,
Please have Ginny come prepared for gym class. Sneakers are a requirement. Socks are not appropriate for outdoor play.
Sincerely,
Mr. Simkins,
Physical Education

Sept. 25

Do you always wear yellow socks?
—B

I'm going to get you Brian Bukvic!!! What did you do with my sneakers?

Coxwell Cable

MELINDA DAVIS
2610 LARK LANE
WOODLAND GLEN, PENNSYLVANIA   18762

DATE   SEPTEMBER 1 - OCTOBER 1

ACCT.#   2385007853285307662

AMOUNT DUE	DATE DUE	AMOUNT ENCLOSED
$43.41	10-15	$.

PLEASE DETACH AND ENCLOSE TOP PORTION WITH PAYMENT

ACCOUNT NUMBER	SERVICE FROM	SERVICE TO	DATE DUE
2385007853285307662	SEPTEMBER 1	OCTOBER 1	OCTOBER 15

DATE	SERVICE/TRANSACTION DESCRIPTION	AMOUNT
9-1	BASIC	29.00
	MOVIE CHANNEL 1,2 + 3	5.00
9-17	PPV VAMPIRE VIXENS ATTACK MANHATTAN	6.95

Who ordered this movie?

AMOUNT DUE $43.41

Not me.
—Henry

you did so, Henry,
Ginny

...NTS RECEIVED AFTER   OCTOBER 1   ARE NOT INCLUDED IN THIS STATEMENT

CREDITS	OTHER CHARGES (SEE ABOVE)	TAX/FEE	AMOUNT DUE
$0.00	+ $0.00	+ $2.46	= $43.41

...Y A (CR) IS A CREDIT OR A CREDIT BALANCE

LY MAIL

ADDRESSEE

NO POSTAGE
NECESSARY
IF MAILED
IN THE
UNITED STATES

PLEASE COME TO THE COUNSELING OFFICE

To: Miss Angelini, HR #212

Please send Ginny to Mrs. Coble's Kindergarten class after next period. Her brother, Jimmy, is insisting on hiding in his cubbyhole unless his sister comes and picks him up. Also, if she can discuss his cape wearing in class, I would greatly appreciate it.

Thank you,

Miss MacIntosh, Guidance Counselor

VAMPIRE VIXENS

205 days till Summer!

#1

Ginny's Book

life Science rots!

I ♡?

★

LOOKIN GOOD

Flower Power

timmy
David

I don't want to make a lot of fuss,
but I'll never sit at the back of the bus.
All the cool kids are sitting there,
you can tell just by looking at their hair.
I hear the seats are nicer in the back
not like the ones up here all cracked.
Just take a look at the window panes.
They don't even steam up when it rains!
It's plain to see they're having fun
Cracking up, giggle fits, every one.
Eighth graders are back there, too.
Up here little kids roam like it's a zoo.
I don't think there's anyone who'd disagree
that the back of the bus is the place to be.
I don't want to make a lot of fuss,
but I wish I could sit at the back of the bus.
My mom says I have to sit in the front
with my little brother. ☹

DATE DUE

APR 2
APR 15

MISTY
OF CHINCOTEAGUE

MISTY OF CHINCOTEAGUE

By MARGUERITE HENRY · Illustra

Ginny Davis:
The following items are overdue. Please return them as soon as possible

Woodland Central School
Overdue Bill Notice

Title: Author: Call Number   Due Date: Fine: Fee:

Misty of Chincoteague   Henry, Marguerite   H3492   09-25   Overdue $2.00
Stormy, Misty's Foal   Henry, Marguerite   H3494   09-25   Overdue $2.00
Black Stallion   Farley, Walter   P2207   09-25   Overdue $2.00
A Very Young Dancer   Krements, Jill   K4811   09-25   Overdue $2.00

Total due: $8.00

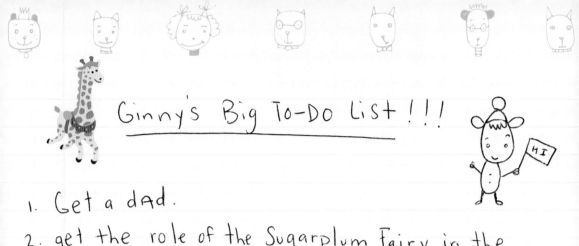

Ginny's Big To-Do List !!!

1. Get a dad.
2. get the role of the Sugarplum Fairy in the Nutcracker.
3. ~~Look good in the school photo for once.~~!!! why bother !!!! (maybe next year)!!
4. ~~Do something with hair to make nose look smaller. Color?? Perm??~~ Leave alone until it grows back !!!!!
5. Win something. Anything.
6. Try to be friends with Mary Catherine Kelly.
7. Get pink sweater back!!
8. Convince mom to let me go see Grampa Joe over Easter break.
9. Get Henry to chill out.
10. Ignore horoscopes whenever possible.

★ ★

11. horseback riding lessons !!!

the sweater

there goes Mary Catherine Kelly
my old best friend
wearing my pink sweater.
It's hard to ignore her,
even though the sweater
looks bad on her —
Pink's just not her color.
She was my best friend
since kindergarten
but not anymore.
Last year I beat her out for a role
in swan lake
and that was it.
She hasn't spoken to
me since except
to say something mean.
There goes mary Catherine Kelly,
my old best friend.
One thing's for sure.
It doesn't look like
I'm getting
that sweater back
any time
soon.

(color)

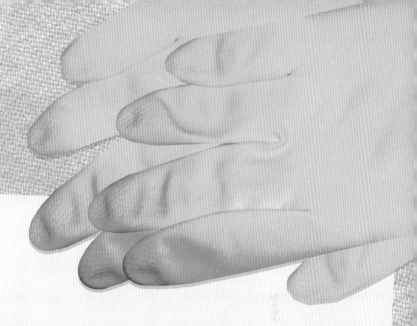

MEMO:

TO: Ginny
FROM: Management (aka Mom)
RE: Sweater

After much consideration, I am willing to purchase
the requested sweater in exchange for dish-washing
duties for one month, or until I can get in a
dishwasher repair man. Kindly sign on the below
line to indicate your consent.

ginny the "Dish Fairy"
<u>Agreed and Accepted</u>

immediately!
<u>Date</u>

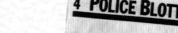

4 POLICE BLOTTER

GNOMES SUSPICIOUSLY VANISH ON PINE STREET

WOODLAND GLEN, PA- The theft of several garden gnomes from the yard of Mr. and Mrs. Noorski has left the neighborhood puzzled. The gnomes, five in all, had been brought over from Norway on a family vacation, and had been a source of pride for many years.

"They were right in the front yard next to the mums when we went to bed," declared Mrs. Noorski.

At this time, the police have no suspects. Foul play is suspected as this is the third reported theft of garden gnomes.

Anybody with any information regarding the theft is asked to please report it to the police department.

stinky poems

GinnyGirl

INSTANT MESSAGE

Current Version: 1.1.0 (Build 1)
Latest Version: 2.5.0 (Build 23)

Guess what? Bob is downstairs right now + he's gonna ask mom 2 get married.

cancel   send

dumbwork

beckysooboo1

INSTANT MESSAGE

Current Version: 1.1.0 (Build 1)
Latest Version: 2.5.0 (Build 23)

no way. how do you know?

cancel   send

GinnyGirl

INSTANT MESSAGE

Current Version: 1.1.0 (Build 1)
Latest Version: 2.5.0 (Build 23)

i just do!!!!!!!!!!!!!!!!!!!!!!!!!!!

cancel   send

nut'n

I found Bob
right on our very own street.
There I was in the driveway
banging a tennis ball
on the garage door
in the middle of
a hot summer day.

bob-mobile

Bob pulled up
next to the curb
in a car that looked like
someone took care of it.
He was an insurance salesman,
he explained, and lost.
I looked into those
big brown trustworthy eyes,
and just knew he'd make
a great dad.
They were the kind of eyes
you would expect
on a golden retriever or maybe
a nice old cat.
I gave him directions,
and then I told him that my mom
could really use some insurance.

LIFE SCIENCE -- LAB 3·8 LIVING THINGS

ginny davis

PROBLEM: What is a living thing?

PURPOSE: To identify a living thing's characteristics.

MATERIALS: environment, iodine

✓+

PROCEDURE:

1. Obtain a mushroom of any kind and look for reproductive organs. Can you find any reproductive organs? *I think so.* They look like spores under the top.

2. What color are they? *white*

3. Is it capable of responding? *According to the book, it can respond to the environment through growth patterns*

4. Test for metabolism and organization by observing it under the microscope and then adding iodine to test for starch. Can you see the cells? *yes*

5. Take the mushroom and let it lie. Does it move? *no*

6. Observe carefully. Did the mushroom adapt well to it's environment? If so, why? *yes because it's brown, and dirt is brown, too, so this means that it's adapted to look like dirt.*

7. Draw your object below:

yuck

CONCLUSION:

1. Does your object sum up as a living thing? *yes*

2. Was there anything remarkable about your mushroom? *no, it's just a plain old mushroom my mom got at the supermarket. It was on sale.*

3. Final comments? *I really hope we're not having mushrooms for dinner tonight.*

Ginny

Mrs. Kurtz called (555-8790). Said she knows you're a busy girl but wondering if you'd reconsider babysitting for Tiffany.

Mom

P.S. She said she'd pay double.

To the Members of the Household—

Attention. Please do not bathe Fluffy and then encourage her to roll in kitty litter. She will not freeze like a statue.

Sincerly, the Management

Hi Becky Soo,
I'm writing this in fourth period and will put it in your purse at lunch. I got my dress for the wedding this weekend. It's lemon yellow. I'm going to be Maid of Honor. I get to carry a bouquet and everything! I'm so excited! I can hardly wait!
Ginny w/B

P.S. Mom says you can be my guest, which would be GREAT because then I wouldn't have to sit with my little brother

Hi Ginny,
Cool! I love yellow It goes with everything. Are you going to try out for the Nutcracker Ballet? I'm pretty sure the Sugarplum Fairy gets to wear a pink tutu (but maybe you could convince Madame Cecile to make it yellow instead!)
Becky Soo

Hi Becky soo,
Yes. Auditions are next month. I really want that part. I've been practicing all summer!!!!!

Henry got sent to the vice principal's office yesterday. My mom says if he doesn't stop dropping cherry bombs down the toilets in school she's going to send him to the military academy. I'm hoping Bob helps things out.

Ginny
P.S. want to go see the new Vampire Vixens movie on Friday??? It's Vampire Vixens Versus the Monster Alligators!!

Suzy's Formals

1 mandarin collar ecru gown	$700.00
1 child's formal dress/lemon yellow	$ 80.00
alterations	$100.00
Subtotal	
Tax	$880.00
Total	$ 52.80
Less deposit	$932.80
	-$400.00
Total	
	$532.00

check payable upon delivery
(checks to be made out to Suzy's Formals)

Thank You!

Dear Mrs. Davis,
Your dress will be available for pick-up next week. I know your daughter has her heart set on yellow, but you might want to consider suggesting that she use dusky rose instead (I've enclosed a swatch). Lemon yellow simply does not match your dress and is not appropriate for an autumn wedding.
Sincerely yours,

Suzy

EXPR— Photo

School Photo Order Form

don't bother!!!!!

Name: Davis, Genevieve
School: Woodland Central
Grade: 7

Photos	Price		Quantity	Total
8.5 x 11	$11.95	each print	___	___
5 x 7	$8.95	each print	___	___
3 x 5	$6.95	each print	___	___
wallet size	$8.95	per sheet of twelve	___	___

Why not? You look sort of cute. Even if your hair is pink.

TOTAL

Order now in time for the holidays!

✂ -

Order no. 22562
Please retain this copy

WOODLAND BANK
"Your Hometown Bank"

ACCOUNT NO.	ACCOUNT TYPE	STATEMENT PERIOD
4357287	WORRY-FREE CHECKING	Sept. 1 - Oct. 1

Genevieve Davis
Melinda Davis (guardian)
2610 Lark Lane
Woodland Glen, PA 18762

Posting Date	Transaction Description	Deposits & Interests	Checks & Subtractions	Daily Balance
9-01	BEGINNING BALANCE			$5.00
9-01	DEPOSIT	+ $25.00		$30.00
9-03	ATM		- $25.00	$5.00
9-05	DEPOSIT	+ $20.00		$25.00
9-07	ATM		- $20.00	$5.00
9-15	DEPOSIT	+ $5.00		$10.00
9-18	DEPOSIT	+ $35.00		$45.00
9-22	ATM		- $40.00	$5.00
9-30	ENDING BALANCE			$5.00

beckysooboo1

INSTANT MESSAGE

Current Version: 1.1.0 (Build 1)
Latest Version: 2.5.0 (Build 23)

do u think your mom will pay 4
horseback riding lessons??

cancel   send

dumbwork

GinnyGirl

INSTANT MESSAGE

Current Version: 1.1.0 (Build 1)
Latest Version: 2.5.0 (Build 23)

she said what she always says.

wait 4 xmas.   I'll have 2

ask my fairy grandfather!

cancel   send

essay #1

poems

Dear Grampa Joe,

How are you? I am fine. School is okay. Not much new here. Becky Soo is going to start taking horseback riding lessons, and I think it would be a great idea if I took them too. They're very good for balance, which is important for me because I'm a ballerina. They're very expensive, though.

Love,

your granddaughter,

Ginny

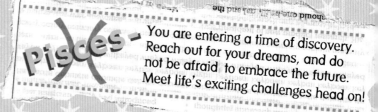

P.S. By the way, I'm going to be the Sugarplum Fairy for Halloween. In case you were wondering.

Pisces – You are entering a time of discovery. Reach out for your dreams, and do not be afraid to embrace the future. Meet life's exciting challenges head on!

NAME: Ginny Davis

DATE: October 16

Life Science Chapter Five Quiz

A-

Please describe fully:

FISSION — the division of a one-celled organism to make two

MICRORGANISM — microscopic living things

PROTIST — a kingdom that has characteristics of plants and animals.

ALGAE — types of protest (sp. protist)

CILIA — tiny hairlike things sticking out all over

FLAGELLUM — a whiplike extension on a protest (sp. protist)

PSEUDOPOD — my brother Timmy who spilled a gallon of milk on my Life Science notes

PHYTON — plant

HABITAT — place where it lives (plant, animal)

The Video Shack

October 29

Rental (VHS) George Balanchine's Nutcracker Ballet $3.95
(New York City Ballet; 1993)

Total $3.95

Each additional night is $1.95.

Be kind! Please rewind!

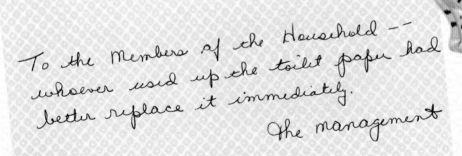

To the Members of the Household -- whoever used up the toilet paper had better replace it immediately.

The management

REPORT CARD

KEY 10 = A+ 9.5 = A 9 = A- 8.5 = B+ 8 = B 7.5 = B- 7 = C+ 6.5 = C 6 = C- 5.5 = D 5 = D- 4.5 = F

COURSE TITLE	ACADEMIC MARKS							ATTENDANCE		CONDUCT CITZ.	CREDITS EARNED	TEACHER COMMENTS
ENGLISH	9	9	10	9	10	10	10					A
MATHEMATICS	8	9	8	8	9	8.5	8.5					B+
SOCIAL STUDIES	9	9.5	9	9	9	9.5	9					A
LIFE SCIENCE	10	8.5	9	10	10	8	9					B+
HEALTH EDUCATION	9.5	10	9	9.5	9.5	10	9					A
ART	5.5	5	5	5	6	6	5.5					C-
PHYS ED	9	10	10	9	9	10	7					A

DAYS ABSENT	0
UNEXCUSED	0
TIMES TARDY	0

TEACHER COMMENTS

Ginny is a pleasure to have in class.

Woodland Central

A recognized school of ex

Dear Parents,

The 7th graders will be given achievement tests on Thursday and Friday.

Results will be available in the spring.

Sincerely,

Mrs. MacGillicuty
Principal

Melinda Davis, Bob Wright a[nd] St. Andrew's Lutheran Chu[rch]

WOODLAND GLEN, PA– Melinda Davis and Bob Wright were married in an afternoon ceremony at St. Andrew's Lutheran Church. The reception was held at the John Adams Inn.

The bride wore a simple tea-length dress of cream silk with a mandarin collar. She carried a spray of gardenias, baby's breath, and stephanotis.

The bride's daughter and maid of honor, Genevieve Davis, wore a dress of bold lemon satin, with puffed sleeves, full hooped skirt, and carried a bouquet of sweetheart roses.

The ring bearer, Timothy Davis, wore a tuxedo accented by an interesting red cape.

The bride, a graduate of Dickenson College, is employed by Carp & Wade Law Associates. The groom works for Life Insurance America.

Attention all Male members of the House

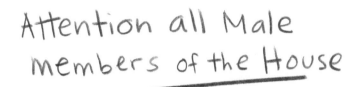

1. Always put seat down on toilet (especially at night)
2. Please do not use my hairbrush on the dog

I'm sure if we follow these simple rules we will all get along.

Thank you. Ginny.

P.S. And hands off my hair spray, Henry!!

 !!

DOGG

Ginny Davis, Period 6

Teacher: Mr. Cusumano

English Assignment: Describe a Change in Your Life

Please be descriptive. 150 -word minimum

A interesting perspective

New Stepdad

My mom just married Mr. Wright.

I really like my new stepdad. We call him Bob. He's pretty cool, and is trying to teach me how to play chess, and he makes really good macaroni and cheese. The homemade kind, not the kind out of the box.

But all of a sudden there are things like razors and shaving cream and something called toe fungus ointment in the bathroom. And while I expected a stepfather to bring some stuff, I never imagined it would be bad habits. For starters, brothers who knew perfectly well how to put the toilet lid down now think it's okay to leave it up. Not to mention, they suddenly think nothing of borrowing my red nail polish to paint Hoover's nails and he's a dog.

So while I'm happy to have a dad around and think that learning chess is kind of cool, I'd be a lot happier not falling into the toilet in the middle of the night.

(164 words)

Madame Cecile's
Ballet Academy

The Nutcracker Ballet Cast

Sugarplum Fairy	Mary Catherine Kelly
Clara	Vicki Timbers
King Rat	Susie Nickerson
Governess	Marisol Cruz
Chinese Dancer	Amy McHugh
Snow Queen	Lizbeth Haws
Nutcracker Prince	Eric Zebraski
Snow King	George Mott
Herr Drosselmeyer	Jack Castara
Arabian	Asher McSnoll

Ensemble (in alphabetical order):

Jill Aaronson
Sara Biedermeyer
Ginny Davis
Sue Figliuolo
Ashley Gottfried
Jacqui Kelly
Mee Kim
Ilene McKay
Sara Patel
Anna Rusins
Gemma Siegel-McDermott
Alexandra Sorge

I think you should get a badge
for not smacking
your bratty little brother
when he eats the charms
off your bracelet because
he thinks it will give
him super powers.

I think you should get a badge
for taking the blame
about shaving the cat
when it was
your weird older brother who did it.

I think you should get a badge
for not crying when
your new stepfather
forgets to pick you up
after school
and Mary Catherine Kelly
gets the part
of the Sugarplum Fairy.

I think you should get a badge
for all these things,
but the Girl Scouts
don't agree with me.

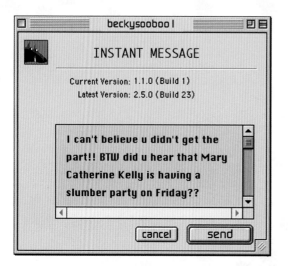

beckysooboo1

INSTANT MESSAGE

Current Version: 1.1.0 (Build 1)
Latest Version: 2.5.0 (Build 23)

I can't believe u didn't get the part!! BTW did u hear that Mary Catherine Kelly is having a slumber party on Friday??

cancel send

photopotamus

dumbwork

GinnyGirl

INSTANT MESSAGE

Current Version: 1.1.0 (Build 1)
Latest Version: 2.5.0 (Build 23)

no. r u invited?

cancel send

coolness

beckysooboo1

INSTANT MESSAGE

Current Version: 1.1.0 (Build 1)
Latest Version: 2.5.0 (Build 23)

yes. r u?

cancel send

oodles of doodles

nut'n

FIVE WAYS

to Shake the Blues!

1. ~~Take a bubble bath!~~ *bad idea!!!!*
2. Listen to a new CD!
3. Buy a cheery plant!
4. Try that new lipstick!
5. Give yourself a facial!

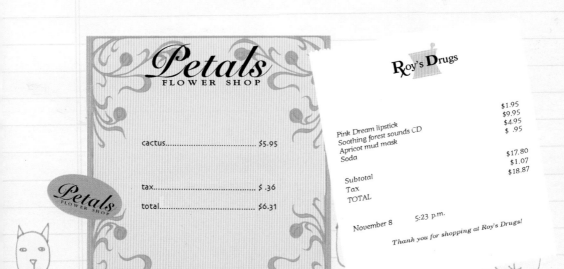

Petals
FLOWER SHOP

cactus.................................... $5.95

tax... $ .36

total....................................... $6.31

Petals
FLOWER SHOP

Thank You! Come Again.

Roy's Drugs

	$1.95
	$9.95
	$4.95
Pink Dream lipstick	$ .95
Soothing forest sounds CD	
Apricot mud mask	
Soda	$17.80
	$1.07
	$18.87
Subtotal	
Tax	
TOTAL	

November 8   5:23 p.m.

Thank you for shopping at Roy's Drugs!

Ginny, my best but
I did my best but.
I think it's ruined.
You should always
check your pockets
before washing
anything. Sorry,
Mom

p.s. Xmas is just
around the corner.

Extra Strength!!

Revolutionary
Stain-Be-Gone!

- **FF-ACTING**
- **WERFUL**
- **RANGE ESSENCE**
- **ID COLOR-SAFE**
- **EACH ALTERNATIVE**
- **MBINE TO FIGHT**
- **OSSIBLE STAINS**
- **U'LL SAY "WOW!"**

℞

N'S HOSPITAL AND REHABILITATION CENTER
WOODLAND GLEN, PENNSYLVANIA
BOK SINGH MD   HARRY J. HOOPIS MD

Cortizone 5 cream.
Use 3 times daily. If
rash persists more than
one week, please call
me. Ginny may be
allergic to apricots.

No more facials.

Dr Singh, MD   M

Look Ginny
it's on again!
(I'll make the
popcorn).

Henry

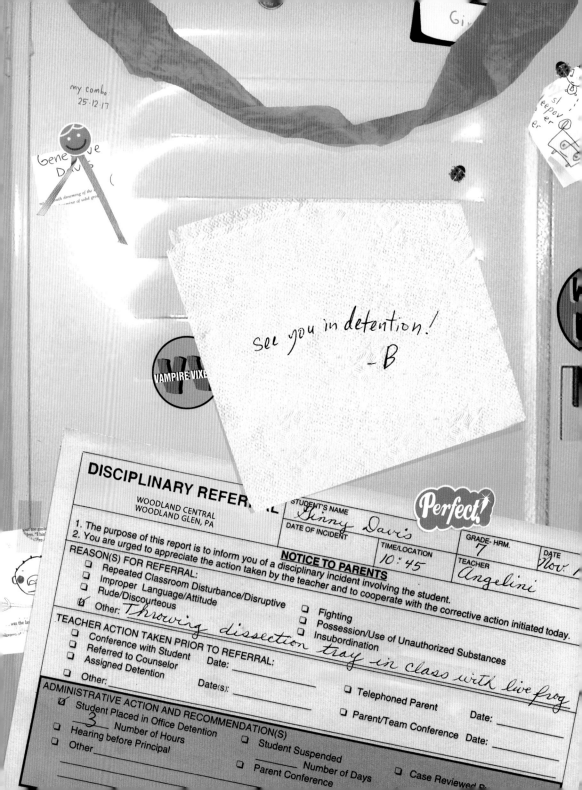

Ginny Davis, Period 6

Teacher: Mr. Cusumano

English Assignment: Describe a Holiday Tradition

Please be descriptive. 150-word minimum

A
very nice!

Pancakes

Every year at Thanksgiving my mom makes pancakes.

This tradition started a long time ago, when my dad was still alive. We made pancakes because my dad always said that having my mom spend a whole day in the kitchen didn't sound like much fun to him.

So, instead, just the five of us would stay home and make pancakes. With all kinds of ingredients like walnuts and strawberries and chocolate-chip bits, which were my favorite. My mom let us make our own pancakes, although sometimes she made some in the shape of Mickey Mouse, which were good, too. After we finished our pancake dinner, we would do something fun like go to the park or race my brother's go-cart down the street or just sit around and watch horror movies.

This year, though, my stepdad, Bob, would like to have a turkey for Thanksgiving, because that's what they always do in his family. And he invited his sister and her husband over for dinner. So now I have to clean my room and the den, help mom fix Thanksgiving dinner, and wear a stupid dress all day.

I wish we were having pancakes.

(196 words)

Ginny's Christmas List

1. sneakers
2. new sweater (gift certificate would be fine)
3. new toe shoes (cash would be fine)
4. Vampire Vixens movie poster and Vampire Vixens comic books #6-9 (I already have #1-5!!)
5. jewelry box (must have lock)

To Whom It May Confuse:

X-mas shopping list

mom - earrings
Bob - something for car
Henry - fireworks
Timmy - new cape??
Grampa Joe - golf clubs
Becky Soo - something horsey

Gobble it up!

GINNY,
TIME TO STUFF
YOURSELF!
   HAPPY THANKSGIVING
GRAMPA JOE
P.S. CAN'T WAIT TO
COME UP AND SEE YOU
IN YOUR BALLET RECITAL!

Eighth graders are stupid,
Becky Soo says.
Her sister who is in the
eighth grade just
had her nose pierced,
her hair dyed purple,
and has been seen behind the bleachers
with some weird kid with a
tattoo of Porky Pig
on his cheek.
And we've all heard the story of
Sara Patel's older sister --
how she drank a wine cooler
on the bus to school and
tried to give her
homeroom teacher a kiss
on the lips. And then,
of course, eighth grade
was the year Henry
started doing dumb things,
like climbing the flagpole naked.
While I've been hearing for years
that eighth graders are stupid it's
never really bothered me before.

But I guess I'm a little worried now.
After all,
I'm going to be an eighth grader next year.

MEMO

TO: All Seventh Graders

FROM: Miss Angelini, Life Science

Due to yesterday's incident, no worms are to be removed and placed in lockers. All worms are to be left in the Life Science lab.

Any student caught removing worms from lab will be given detention.

Thank you for your cooperation.

389 229 360
740

boy you can scream loud!
Brian

for
Miss Angelini

Dear Miss Angelini,
    Please excuse Ginny from school
today. There was a rather unfortunate
accident involving her brother
using her hairbrush on the family
dog and now it appears as if
she has some fleas.
    We are taking her to get dipped.
        Mrs. Davis-Wright

SUGARPLUM FAIRY LIGHT AS AIR

WOODLAND GLEN, PA- The Nutcracker Ballet opened to resounding success with young Mary Catherine Kelly in the role of Sugarplum Fairy. The annual much-anticipated performance was produced in conjunction with Madame Cecile's Ballet Academy. "Miss Kelly is the best Sugarplum Fairy we have ever had," gushed Mrs. Cecile Zabraski, owner of Madame Cecile's Ballet Academy. A standing ovation greeted Miss Kelly's performance.

"I live for ballet," Miss Kelly declared with a gracious smile, accepting a bouquet of roses from an adoring fan.

The Nutcracker will run through to December 24. Tickets are available at the box office.

Madame Cecile's Ballet Academy

FRIDAY
DECEMBER 15
7:30 PM
at the
ALUMNI HALL

Ticket Price: $1
GENERAL ADMISS

Madame Cecile's Ballet Academy

FRIDAY
DECEMBER 15
7:30 PM
at the
ALUMNI HALL

Ticket Price: $10.00
GENERAL ADMISSION

Ginny,
cheer up!
Things could 🐝 worse.
You could be the donkey in
the Christmas Pageant
like Timmy.
Mom

STUDENT: DAVIS, GENEVIEVE
TEACHER: ANGELINI
QUARTER: 2

REPORT CARD

COURSE TITLE	ACADEMIC MARKS							ATTENDANCE	CONDUCT / CITZ.	CREDITS EARNED	TEACHER COMMENTS
KEY 10 = A+ 9.5 = A 9 = A- 8.5 = B+ 8 = B 7.5 = B- 7 = C+ 6.5 = C 6 = C- 5.5 = D 5 = D- 4.5 = F											A
ENGLISH	9	10	10	9	9	10	9				B
MATHEMATICS	8	8	8	8	8.5	8.5	8				A+
SOCIAL STUDIES	10	10	9	9	9	9	9				A-
LIFE SCIENCE	8.5	9	9	8.5	9	9	7.5				A-
HEALTH EDUCATION	9	9	9	9	8.5	8.5	9				C
ART	7	7	7	7	7	7	6				A-
PHYS. ED	10	9	10	9	8.5	8.5	8.5				
DAYS ABSENT									2		
UNEXCUSED									0		
TIMES TARDY									2		

TEACHER COMMENTS

I was surprised to learn that Ginny's brother is a pseudopod.

COURSE

LIFE SCIENCE

Melinda Davis-Wright
Parent's Signature

Ginny,
a "C" is still
unacceptable
in art.
Mom

But at least
it's better
than a C—!!!
♡ Ginny
xoxo

WOODLAND BANK
"Your Hometown Bank"

ACCOUNT NO.	ACCOUNT TYPE	STATEMENT PERIOD
4357287	WORRY - FREE CHECKING	Nov. 1 - Dec. 1

Genevieve Davis
Melinda Davis-Wright (guardian)
2610 Lark Lane
Woodland Glen, PA 18762
Ill......Il.Il....Il.I....I..Il.I.I.I..I.Il.

Posting Date	Transaction Description	Deposits & Interests	Checks & Subtractions	Daily Balance
				$5.00
	BEGINNING BALANCE			$30.00
11-01	DEPOSIT	+ $25.00		$5.00
11-04	ATM		– $25.00	$30.00
11-07	DEPOSIT	+ $25.00		$5.00
11-11	ATM		– $25.00	$30.00
11-14	DEPOSIT	+ $25.00		$5.00
11-18	ATM			$30.00
11-18	DEPOSIT	+ $25.00		$5.00
11-25	ATM		– $25.00	$5.00
11-27	ENDING BALANCE			
11-30				

$$-4.74 = 26¢$$

To Whom It May Confuse:

⭐ <u>X-mas shopping list</u>

mom - ~~earrings~~ rose bubblebath/soap set ($9.95)
Bob - ~~something for car~~ soap-on-a-rope ($5.95)
Henry - ~~fireworks~~ aftershave ($4.89)
Timmy - new ~~cape??~~ ducky soap ($3.25)
Grampa Joe - ~~golf clubs~~ shaving set ($10.95)
Becky Soo - ~~something horsey~~ watermelon bubblebath
                                                    (have)

mom -
If mrs. Kurtz calls,
tell her I'll babysit
Tiffany.

⭐

Ginny ⭐

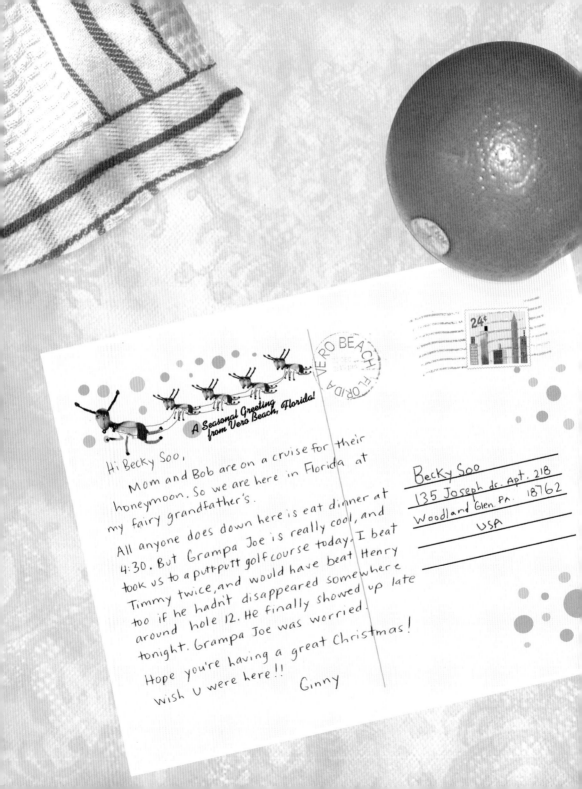

A Seasonal Greeting from Vero Beach, Florida!

VERO BEACH FLORIDA

24¢

Hi Becky Soo,

Mom and Bob are on a cruise for their honeymoon. So we are here in Florida at my fairy grandfather's.

All anyone does down here is eat dinner at 4:30. But Grampa Joe is really cool, and took us to a putt-putt golf course today. I beat Timmy twice, and would have beat Henry too if he hadn't disappeared somewhere around hole 12. He finally showed up late tonight. Grampa Joe was worried.

Hope you're having a great Christmas! Wish U were here!!

Ginny

Becky Soo
135 Joseph dr. Apt. 218
Woodland Glen, Pa. 18762
USA

'Twas the Night before Christmas

(Ginny version)

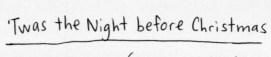

'Twas the night before Xmas
And all through the retirement community
Not a creature was stirring,
Not even my brother Henry.
The cicadas were chirping
    In the warm Florida air
And Timmy was running around
In his red cape and underwear.
The presents were stacked
Next to the ceramic tree
And I noticed a few tags
That said "From Santa to Ginny."
The children were not nestled
All snug in their beds,
Not with visions of presents
Dancing in their heads!
We begged and begged to open just one box
And finally Grampa Joe said, sure, why not?
Then what to my wandering eye should appear?
But the most perfect pink sweater so soft and dear!
Grampa Joe! I cried, you're the best fairy Grandfather ever!
Now I'll be warm, no matter the weather.
But Grampa Joe just smiled, gave a wink, and said,
Did I mention I rented Vampire Vixens Versus the Zombie Undead?

Police Blotter
RASH OF WHEEL STEALS

VERO BEACH, FL- Residents of the Royal Retirement community are baffled by a rash of wheelchair disappearances. The wheelchairs are apparently taken from resident's porches during the night.

"I thought I saw a tire rim in the swamp by the golf course," said Abe Sanders. "Then again, maybe it was nothing. Whoever's taking them could be selling them. There's a big market for wheelchairs down here, you know."

Residents are urged to keep wheelchairs indoors.

If you have any information regarding the whereabouts of the wheelchairs, please contact Bert MacKenzie in the Royal Palms Security Office.

January 3

Dear Mr. and Mrs. Davis-Wright,

Thank you very much for the thoughtful Christmas gift. I never have enough paperweights. And shaped like an apple, too!! How clever! It is a wonderful feeling to know that we are appreciated.

It is a pleasure to have Ginny in class. You can tell she is loved by the openness she displays in her opinions.

Sincerely,
Caroline Angelini

SPEEDY TELEGRAPH MESSAGING SERVICE
"blink and it's there"

HI KIDS. STOP. WE ARE HAVING FUN. STOP. HOPE YOU ARE NOT DRIVING GRAMPA NUTS. STOP. SEE YOU AFTER NEW YEAR'S. STOP. GINNY, DO NOT LET HENRY FEED YOUR LITTLE BROTHER TO THE ALLIGATORS ON THE GOLF COURSE. STOP. THAT GOES FOR YOU, TOO. STOP. LOVE MOM AND BOB. STOP.

Ginny's New Year's Resolutions!!!

1. Try harder to be nice to Bob.
2. Focus on ballet. Advanced toe-shoe lessons. Find other transportation.
3. Get a lead role in Swan Lake.
4. Get a date for the Spring Fling.
5. Do something with hair to make nose look smaller.
6. Win something. Anything.
7. Try harder to be friends with Mary Catherine Kelly.
8. Have a cool birthday party.
9. Really get Henry to chill out.
10. Ignore horoscopes whenever possible!!!
11. Do not babysit for the kurtzes no matter how poor!!!

Point out th.
heart set on to

PISCES
February 19–March 20
Exciting times are approaching, dear Pisces. Take this opportunity to lay new plans for the coming year. You are the star of your own life!

Welcome back to a new year!

As a requirement for graduation of seventh grade, you will all be required to make a project for the science fair to be held in May. Please fill out the attached form outlining the scope of your project.

Sincerely,

Miss Angelini

Madame Cecile's
Ballet Academy

Announcement

Tryouts for the Spring Recital of
Swan Lake
to be held March 1
promptly at 4:00 p.m.

Swan Lake
TCHAIK
TCHAIKOVSKY

SNACS
RC BOOKSTORE
NO REFUND IF REMOVED
U$ 4.99

ESSENTIAL SWAN LAKE

**The Life and Ballet
of Lev Ivanov**

**CHOREOGRAPHER OF
THE NUTCRACKER
AND SWAN LAKE**

by Roland John Wiley

Feb

mon	tue	wed	thu	fri
			1	2
5	6	7	8	9
1	12	13	14 ♥	15	16
18	19	20	21	22 Ginny's Bday

WORD A DAY IS A GOOD WAY TO PLAY!

love
cuteboys
kind

Answers to previous puzzle

ASHLEY COSTA

Ideas For Ginny's 13th Birthday Party

1. Party at Disney World ←✈
2. Space Camp 🚀
3. Go to Transylvania to see Vampire Vixens   *nice try*
4. Trip to New York City to see ballet!!!!

what about a slumber party?
Mom

Quarter Science Project   Name: Ginny D

Project: I will make a replica of the human brain.

Great idea! I can hardly wait to see it! You should also name the appropriate parts. I can lend you a book if you need it.

Miss Angelini

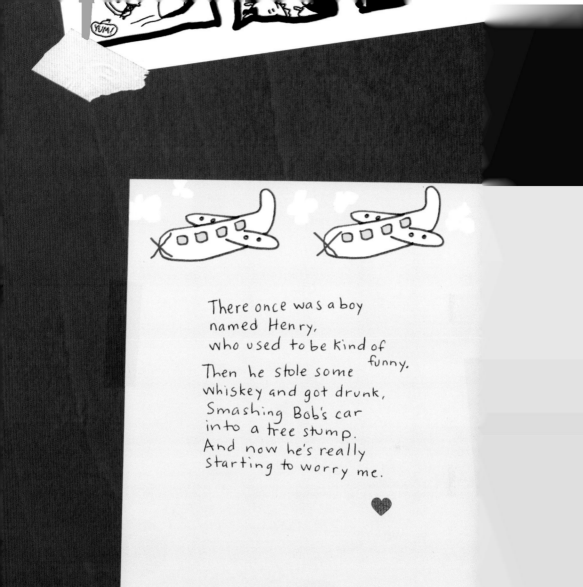

There once was a boy
named Henry,
who used to be kind of
funny.
Then he stole some
whiskey and got drunk,
Smashing Bob's car
into a tree stump.
And now he's really
starting to worry me.

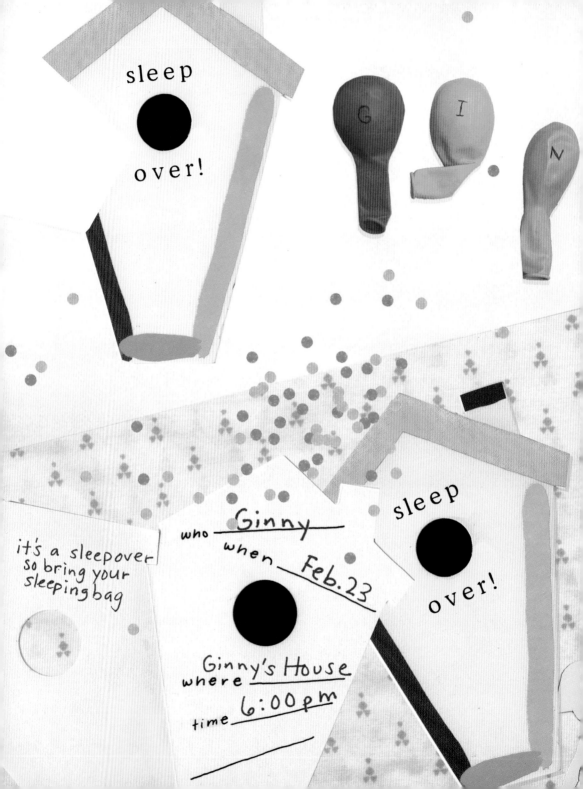

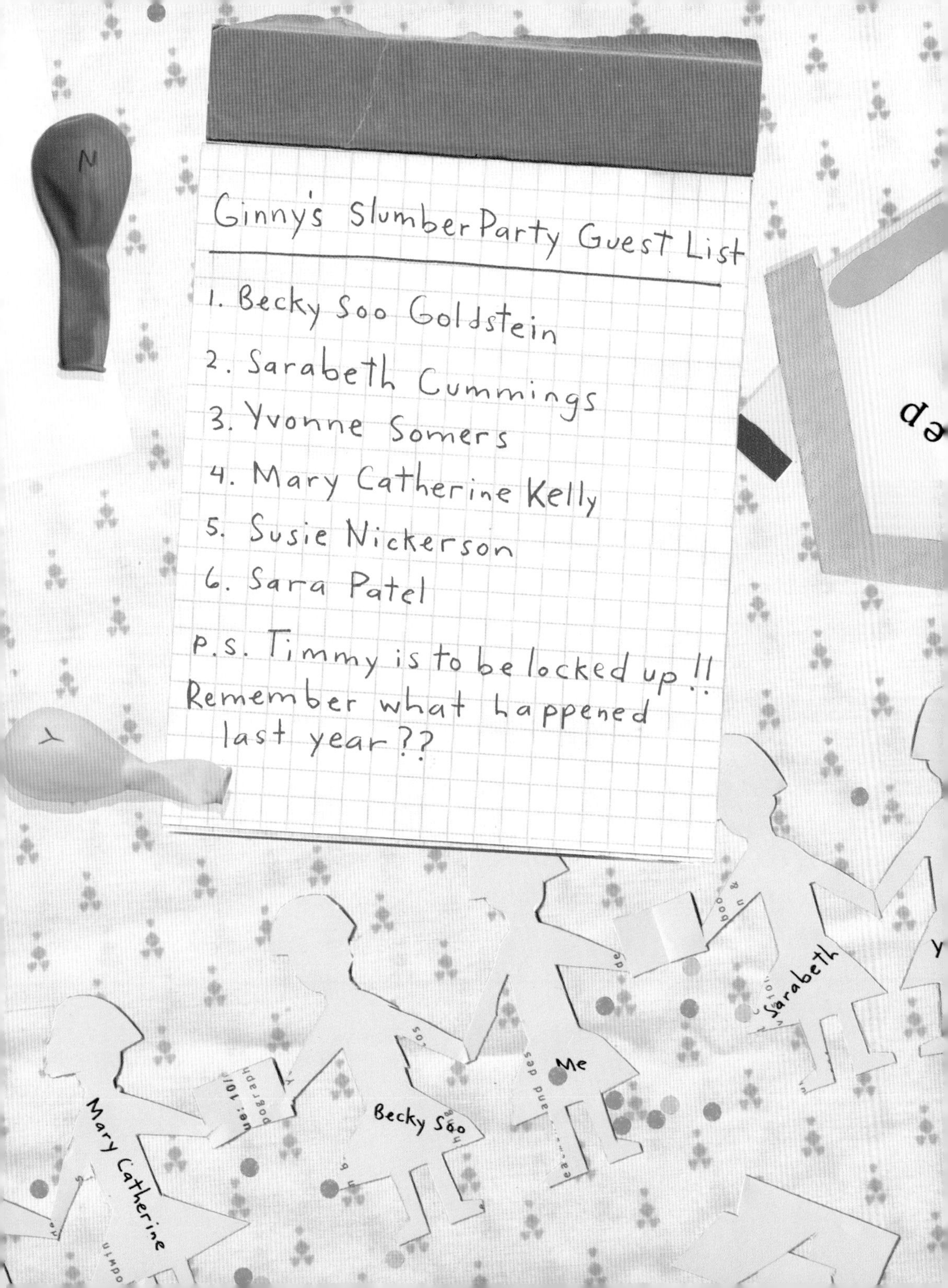

Ginny's Slumber Party Guest List
1. Becky Soo Goldstein
2. Sarabeth Cummings
3. Yvonne Somers
4. Mary Catherine Kelly
5. Susie Nickerson
6. Sara Patel
P.S. Timmy is to be locked up!! Remember what happened last year??
Mary Catherine
Becky Soo
Me
Sarabeth

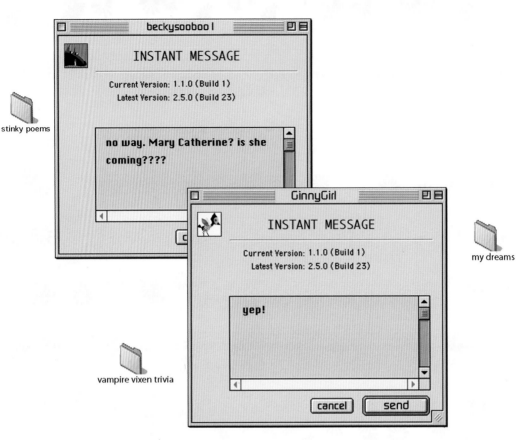

stinky poems

my dreams

vampire vixen trivia

poems

stupid homework

An Ode to the Dumbest Age of All

Oh, the dumbest age of all is
    twelve.
  Too young to drive,
but too old to have your
    parents take you
    to the movies.
Too young to work at
    the mall,
  but too old to
get an allowance anymore.
Too young to stay up to
  watch television,
but old enough to babysit
    your bratty little
    brother.
Oh, the dumbest age of all is
    twelve.
  I'm just hoping that
  thirteen isn't so dumb.

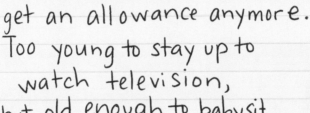

Happy Birthday

Happy Birthday to a
real teenager!
Love,
Mom + Bob

To my special
Granddaughter
on her Birthday

HAPPY BIRTHDAY !
MAY ALL YOUR ~~FISHES~~
WISHES COME TRUE.
GRAMPA JOE

(P.S. YOU DON'T THINK YOUR BROTHER HENRY TOOK
THOSE WHEELCHAIRS BY ANY CHANCE, DO YOU?)

Hey Brat! You're 13 now.
Only 2 years until you
get your driving permit
and can crash into a
tree like me! Ha-Ha!
Your brother, H

Happy Birthday
love Henry--

Happy Birthday
Ginny!
FROM : TIMMY

Ginny Davis, Period 6

Teacher: Mr. Cusumano

English Assignment: Describe a Tragic Incident in Your Life

Please be descriptive. 200 - word minimum

A

Thirteenth Birthday

I used to think that the worst thing that ever happened to me was my dad dying when I was just a little kid and having every single grown-up I met say, "You *poor thing.*"

But then I grew up and realized that the worst thing of all is inviting your friends over for a slumber party and having your little brother show up wearing his dumb red cape and run around screaming and then watching your new stepdad come thundering down the stairs, hair sticking out in all directions, orange polka-dot boxer shorts flapping, and yell that it's late, and he doesn't care if it's a birthday party because he has to get up at six a.m. to catch a flight.

And that's when I realized that things couldn't possibly get any worse.

(I have no idea how many words)

english

Mary Catherine told me that your dad has really stupid boxer shorts. Brian

stinky poems

stuff

essay #1

vampire vixen trivia

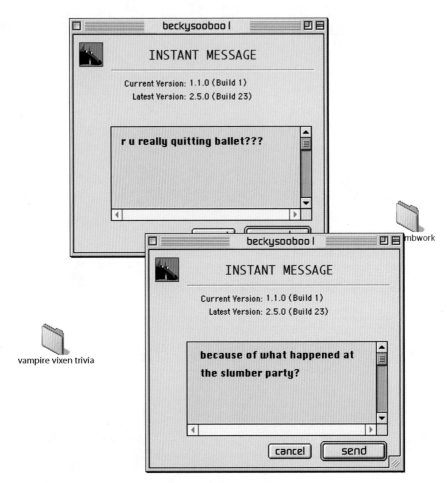

beckysooboo I

INSTANT MESSAGE

Current Version: 1.1.0 (Build 1)
Latest Version: 2.5.0 (Build 23)

r u really quitting ballet???

mbwork

beckysooboo I

INSTANT MESSAGE

Current Version: 1.1.0 (Build 1)
Latest Version: 2.5.0 (Build 23)

because of what happened at the slumber party?

cancel send

beckysooboo I

INSTANT MESSAGE

Current Version: 1.1.0 (Build 1)
Latest Version: 2.5.0 (Build 23)

Ginny!!!!! Who cares what Mary Catherine says!!

cancel send

poems

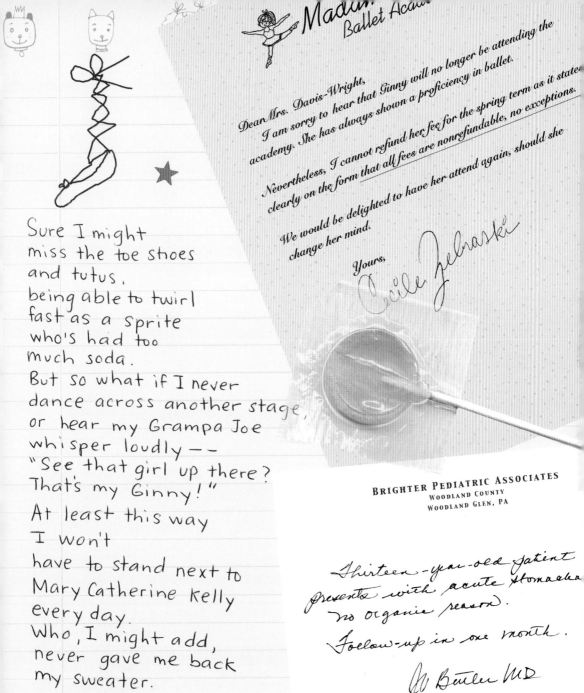

Madam...
Ballet Acad...

Sure I might
miss the toe shoes
and tutus.
being able to twirl
fast as a sprite
who's had too
much soda.
But so what if I never
dance across another stage,
or hear my Grampa Joe
whisper loudly —
"See that girl up there?
That's my Ginny!"
At least this way
I won't
have to stand next to
Mary Catherine Kelly
every day.
Who, I might add,
never gave me back
my sweater.

BRIGHTER PEDIATRIC ASSOCIATES
WOODLAND COUNTY
WOODLAND GLEN, PA

Thirteen-year-old patient
presents with acute stomach
no organic reason.
Follow-up in one month.

JV Butler MD

assignm t:

Sketch   object using shading and highlights.

Genevieve Davis

there's something sort of nice
about the way a pencil
can smudge across a paper
like a fuzzy blanket

how one little v
can look like a bird
flying above an ocea

Drawing's not like ballet
where everything has
to be perfect
no matter what.

Not to mention
there's something to
be said for being able
to erase mistakes.

GINNY
    WHY DON'T YOU COME BY
DURING YOUR STUDY HALL
AND I'LL GIVE YOU SOME
POINTERS?
            Mrs Willis

Notes on Human ~~Brian~~ Brain for
Science Project

brain has nerve cells called <u>neurons</u>!
<u>Brain parts</u> in most animals and humans

1. ~~Brainstem~~ - reflexes, movement,
   and functions, like heart
   rate, blood pressure, digestion,
   urination (gross!)
2. ~~Cerebellum~~ - coordinates stuff
3. ~~Hypothalamus~~ and ~~pituitary gland~~
   body temperature and behavior.
4. ~~Cerebrum~~ and ~~cortex~~ does everything else.

Brains in animals...
some animals do not have <u>real</u> brains.
   a. ~~Flatworms~~ have neural nets,
   not real brains (which is good
   because they seem pretty dumb)
   b. ~~Lobsters~~ have "simple" brains
   made up of neural nets called
   ~~ganglia~~
             (I don't know about this --
             the lobster that mom cooked
             that time looked like ~~he~~ it
             knew what was going to
             happen!)
   c. 🙂 ~~Brian Bukvic~~ has no brains
                                    at all.

GOTCHA!

Sorry I'm broke
want to go shoplift
some candy?

H—

NICE GIRL

To: Jimmy
Don't be sad,
Don't be blue
This valentine
Is just for you!

Susie
For: Jimmy

IT'S LOVE

LOVE HER

TRUE LOVE

BE MY HERO

uts
about
you!

FOR MY FAVORITE
GRANDDAUGHTER, STAY
AWAY FROM THOSE
PIMPLY BOYS!
♡ GRAMP
JO

For
prrr
daug

I'M SURE

Hey
banana nose —
you better keep an eye on
your sneakers!
guess who?

TRUE LOVE

NICE GIRL

PARSONS AND ROMANO ORTHODONTICS

WILLIAM B. PARSONS, DMD   ARNOLD S. ROMANO, DMD

Dear Mrs. Davis-Wright,

As I suspected, Genevieve will need braces. Please call my office for an appointment to discuss.

Sincerely,

William B. Parsons, DMD

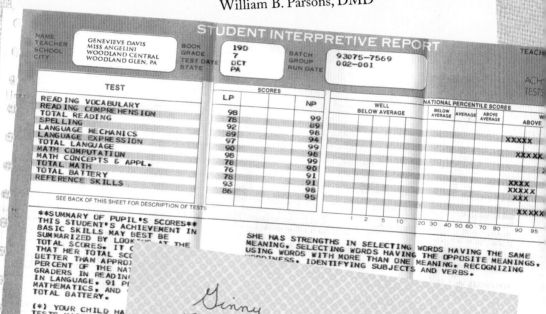

STUDENT INTERPRETIVE REPORT

NAME	GENEVIEVE DAVIS
TEACHER	MISS ANGELINI
SCHOOL	WOODLAND CENTRAL
CITY	WOODLAND GLEN, PA

BOOK	19D
GRADE	7
TEST DATE	OCT
STATE	PA

BATCH	93075-7569
GROUP	002-001
RUN DATE	

TEST	LP	NP
READING VOCABULARY	98	99
READING COMPREHENSION	78	89
TOTAL READING	92	98
SPELLING	89	94
LANGUAGE MECHANICS	97	99
LANGUAGE EXPRESSION	90	98
TOTAL LANGUAGE	98	99
MATH COMPUTATION	78	90
MATH CONCEPTS & APPL.	76	91
TOTAL MATH	78	98
TOTAL BATTERY	93	95
REFERENCE SKILLS	86	

SEE BACK OF THIS SHEET FOR DESCRIPTION OF TESTS

SUMMARY OF PUPIL'S SCORES
THIS STUDENT'S ACHIEVEMENT IN BASIC SKILLS MAY BEST BE SUMMARIZED BY LOOKING AT THE TOTAL SCORES. IT C... THAT HER TOTAL SCO... BETTER THAN APPROX... PERCENT OF THE NATI... GRADERS IN READING... IN LANGUAGE, 91 P... MATHEMATICS, AND ... TOTAL BATTERY.

(*) YOUR CHILD HA... TESTS MARKED BY A...

SHE HAS STRENGTHS IN SELECTING WORDS HAVING THE SAME MEANING, SELECTING WORDS HAVING THE OPPOSITE MEANINGS, USING WORDS WITH MORE THAN ONE MEANING, RECOGNIZING WORDINESS, IDENTIFYING SUBJECTS AND VERBS.

DEAR TEACHER:

You are being pro... Report for each ch... to assist you in pl... students.

A third copy ... form parents ... skills.

Ginny
For a girl who's so good at understanding words, you sure do seem to have a lot of problems understanding "Clean Up Your Room"
Mom

P.S. what's that strange smell coming from under your bed? It better not be the leftover pizza from last week.

WOODLAND BANK
"Your Hometown Bank"

ACCOUNT NO.	ACCOUNT TYPE	STATEMENT PERIOD
4357287	WORRY-FREE CHECKING	Feb. 1 - Mar. 1

Genevieve Davis
Melinda Davis-Wright (guardian)
2610 Lark Lane
Woodland Glen, PA 18762
llmmllllmllldmldlldldmllll

Posting Date	Transaction Description	Deposits & Interests	Checks & Subtractions	Daily Balance
				$5.00
				$30.00
2-01	BEGINNING BALANCE	+ $25.00		$5.00
2-04	DEPOSIT		– $25.00	$30.00
2-07	ATM	+ $25.00		$5.00
2-11	DEPOSIT		– $25.00	$30.00
2-14	ATM	+ $25.00		$5.00
2-18	DEPOSIT		– $25.00	$30.00
2-18	ATM	+ $25.00		$5.00
2-25	DEPOSIT		– $25.00	$5.00
2-27	ATM			$5.00
2-29	ENDING BALANCE			

C K M

Dear Mrs. Davis-Wright,
    This is to inform you that we will not be requiring Ginny's babysitting services anymore.

    I highly doubt that the injury to your daughter's nose was caused by Tiffany biting it. Tiffany is simply too old to do something like that.

    I will not be recommending your daughter to any of the other parents in the neighborhood.

Sincerely,
Cecilia Kurtz

Roy's **D**rugs

Soda	$ .95
Chocolate (assorted/box)	$15.00
Subtotal	$15.95
Tax	$ .96
TOTAL	$16.91

March 8   6:25 pm

Thank you for shopping at R...

What To Do When You've Hit Bottom

1. Pamper yourself with a bubble bath!
2. Paint your nails!
3. Color your hair a new shade for spring!
4. Try a sassy new lipstick!
5. Dazzle things up with sparkly hair clips!

hey banana nose!
looking good!!

Dear Mrs. Davis-Wright,

I am very sorry to hear that your Aunt Martha died.

Please accept my condolences, and I will be happy to arrange to send Ginny's homework home with one of her friends if you'd like.

Tell Ginny that she is in our prayers.

Kind regards,
Caroline Angelini

Ginny —
Who's Aunt Martha?
Mom
p.s. This better
   be good!

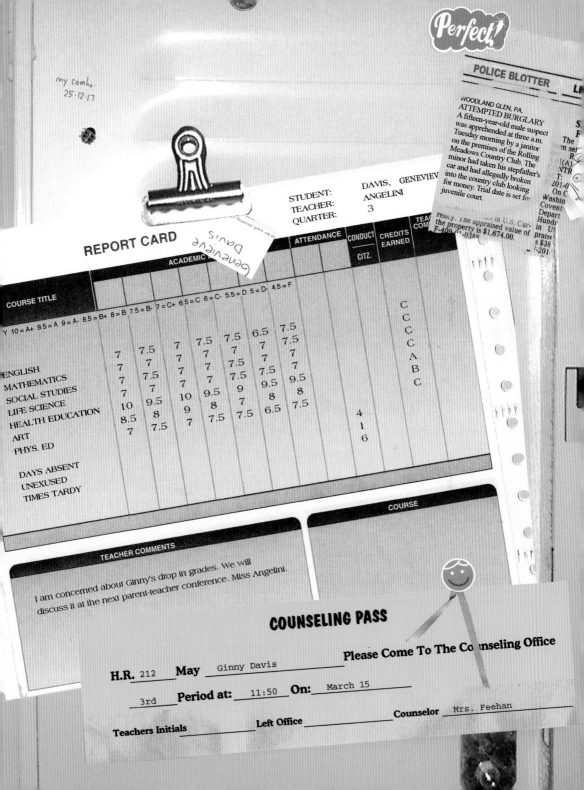

my combo:
25-12-17

Perfect!

STUDENT: DAVIS, GENEVIEVE ANGELINI
TEACHER:
QUARTER: 3

REPORT CARD

Genevieve Davis

ACADEMIC

COURSE TITLE									ATTENDANCE	CONDUCT CITZ.	CREDITS EARNED

Y 10 = A+ 9.5 = A 9 = A- 8.5 = B+ 8 = B 7.5 = B- 7 = C+ 6.5 = C 6 = C- 5.5 = D 5 = D- 4.5 = F

Course								Citz.	Credits
ENGLISH	7	7.5	7	7.5	7.5	6.5	7.5	C	
MATHEMATICS	7	7	7	7	7	7	7.5	C	
SOCIAL STUDIES	7	7.5	7	7	7.5	7	7	C	
LIFE SCIENCE	7	7	7	9.5	9	9.5	9.5	C	
HEALTH EDUCATION	10	9.5	10	8	7	8	8	A	
ART	8.5	8	9	7.5	7.5	6.5	7.5	B	4
PHYS. ED	7	7.5	7					C	16
DAYS ABSENT									
UNEXUSED									
TIMES TARDY									

COURSE

TEACHER COMMENTS

I am concerned about Ginny's drop in grades. We will discuss it at the next parent-teacher conference. Miss Angelini.

COUNSELING PASS

Please Come To The Counseling Office

H.R. 212 **May** Ginny Davis

3rd **Period at:** 11:50 **On:** March 15

Teachers Initials _____ **Left Office** _____ **Counselor** Mrs. Feehan

What happened to Henry

I heard him sneak out

the back door creaking because no one ever oils it.

ruff

I heard Hoover whine to be petted because Henry's his favorite human.

I even heard the car back out the driveway, thinking it was just another silly prank.

I just never thought he'd do something THat would make my stepfather

Shout and turn red and my mother cry and cry and cry.

I guess I should've known and stopped him.

but I didn't.

DISCIPLINARY REFERRAL

WOODLAND CENTRAL
WOODLAND GLEN, PA

STUDENT'S NAME		GRADE- HRM.	DATE
Genevieve Davis		7	3-18
DATE OF INCIDENT	TIME/LOCATION	TEACHER	
	12:30	Angelini	

NOTICE TO PARENTS

1. The purpose of this report is to inform you of a disciplinary incident involving the student.
2. You are urged to appreciate the action taken by the teacher and to cooperate with the corrective action initiated today.

REASON(S) FOR REFERRAL:

- ☐ Repeated Classroom Disturbance/Disruptive
- ☐ Improper Language/Attitude
- ☐ Rude Discourteous
- ☑ Other: _slapping another student_
- ☐ Fighting
- ☐ Possession/Use of Unauthorized Substances
- ☐ Insubordination

☐ Telephoned Parent   Date: _____

☐ Parent/Team Conference   Date: _____

TEACHER ACTION TAKEN PRIOR TO REFERRAL:

- ☐ Conference with Student   Date: _____
- ☐ Referred to Counselor   Date(s): _____
- ☐ Assigned Detention
- ☐ Other: _____

☐ Case Reviewed By: _____

ADMINISTRATIVE ACTION AND RECOMMENDATION(S)

- ☑ Student Placed in Office Detention
  - 3   Number of Hours
- ☐ Hearing before Principal
- ☐ Other _____
- ☐ Student Suspended
  - _____ Number of Days
- ☐ Parent Conference

WHITE, Parents' Copy   CANARY, Teacher's Copy   BUFF, Office Copy

I would've slapped
Mary Catherine Kelly, too,
if she'd said that about
my brother.
~B

Ginny,
Bob and I should be back from taking Henry to the military academy some time after five.

Get a pizza from Al's for you and Timmy.

Love,
Mom

p.s. If you need anything, call us on the cell or go next door to Mrs. Whitaker's house.

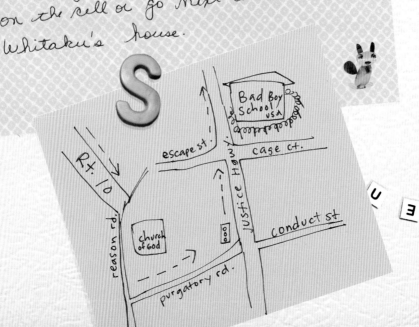

Somebody threw up
in the hallway outside
Miss Macintosh's room.
It's right out there
on the linoleum floor
all covered in sawdust
the janitor put down.
Everyone's talking,
wondering who did it.
If it was Victor Banerjee or
Stacie Epstein or maybe even
Thomas Trout?
It's pretty hard to say.
I just hope they don't find out
it was me.

Ginny's New Year's Resolutions!!!

1. ~~Try harder to be nice to Bob.~~
2. Focus ~~on ballet.~~ Advanced toe-shoe ~~lessons. Find other transportation.~~
3. Get ~~a lead~~ role in Swan Lake.
4. ~~Get a date for the Spring fling.~~
5. ~~Do something~~ ~~with hair to make~~ ~~nose look smaller.~~
6. ~~Win something. Anything.~~
7. ~~Try harder to be~~ friends with Mary Catherine Kelly.
8. ~~Have a cool birthday party.~~
9. ~~Really~~ ~~get~~ ~~Henry to chill out.~~
10. ~~Ignore horoscopes~~ ~~whenever possible!!~~
11. ~~Do not babysit for the Kurtzes~~ no matter how poor!!!

don't bother!!......!!

stinky poems

beckysooboo1

INSTANT MESSAGE

Current Version: 1.1.0 (Build 1)
Latest Version: 2.5.0 (Build 23)

u okay?

cancel   send

dumbwork

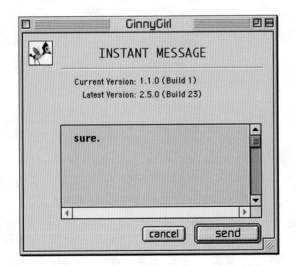

GinnyGirl

INSTANT MESSAGE

Current Version: 1.1.0 (Build 1)
Latest Version: 2.5.0 (Build 23)

sure.

cancel   send

essay??

nut'n

I'm going to be late again.
The alarm went off
but I hit the snooze
button.
  It just seemed easier to
flip over, snuggle down,
and get back to all those
good dreams when I was little
We're at the beach.
  Henry's burying me in sand
and Mom's giggling,
with Timmy in her belly.
My dad's there, too, laughing
his great deep laugh
There's my Ginny Girl!
He tosses me into the waves,
  but I don't care
because my life is
one big smile.
Not like now with
everyone pretending
that Henry never lived
here and Bob always did.
There goes my alarm again
Think I'll dream some more

Horizon Telephone Co.

Account Name: Melinda Davis-Wright
Service User: Melinda Davis-Wright

Telephone Number: 604-555-1975 Account Number: 09202002

Long Distance Calls Date of Invoice: 3/15

Date	Time	Number Called	Calls To	Minutes	Total
02-01	5:04pm	702-555-0143	Discipline Hills, VT	5	$.30
02-03	7:00pm	305-555-0218	Vero Beach, FL	15	$1.30
02-03	4:55pm	702-555-0143	Discipline Hills, VT	5	$.30
02-06	1:30am	305-555-0218	Vero Beach, FL	66	$11.80
02-11	1:13am	305-555-0218	Vero Beach, FL	104	$12.05
02-11	6:42pm	305-555-0218	Vero Beach, FL	22	$1.65
02-12	12:56am	305-555-0218	Vero Beach, FL	93	$12.00
02-12	3:44pm	305-555-0218	Vero Beach, FL	18	$1.75
02-15	3:39pm	305-555-0218	Vero Beach, FL	12	$1.50
02-15	5:37pm	305-555-0218	Vero Beach, FL	36	
02-15	5:37pm	305-555-0218	Vero Beach, FL		
02-17	5:35pm	305-555-	Vero Beach, FL		

Honeycup,
Are you all right?
Let's talk.
Love,
Mom

GINNY
SOME BUNNY WISHES YOU A HOPPY EASTER!
                                I'M LOOKING
                          FORWARD TO YOUR VISIT!
                                    LOVE GRAMPA
                                         JOE
              PS
              I'LL MEET YOU AT THE AIRPORT
              (I'LL BE THE BALD, OLD GUY-HA-HA)

BOARDING PASS
TIKT BP_2F_J/BOS
DAVIS, GINNY
PHILADELPHIA, PA
WEST PALM BEACH, FLA
STURDY AIRLINES INC.
FLIGHT NO. 121
B4   10:88 A.M.   4F   NO
DEPART: 10:30 a.m.
ARRIVE: 1:08 p.m.

I Ate Florida!

Hi Henry,
I'm visiting Grampa Joe for Easter break. It's really hot here. Grampa said to tell you he sent you a box of oranges that you should get real soon. Did you get the box of candy I sent you? Grampa Joe's teaching me how to play poker. I beat the old lady next door.
I miss you. Write me!!!
            Ginny
P.S. Doesn't this alligator look like the alligator from the <u>Vampire Vixens</u> movie?

Attn: Henry Davis
B.B. School of America
114 Justice Hwy
Redemption, VT   03401

9 ♣

HOW TO KEEP A POKER FACE

by Grampa Joe

1. Be calm.
2. Never show your hand.
3. Look straight ahead.
4. Don't blink a lot (makes you look like you're hiding something).
5. Smile, but don't be too nice.
6. If someone challenges you, it probably means they are already losing.
7. Never forget who your opponent is.
8. Don't get upset.
9. Remember that Mary Catherine Kelly is a mean little girl.
10. Don't tell your mother I'm teaching you to gamble or she'll kill me.

list of poker hands

Royal Flush - Ace, King, Queen, Jack and 10, all of the same suit

Straight Flush- Any five-card sequence in the same suit

Four of a Kind- All four cards of the same value

Full House- Three of a kind combined with a pair

Flush- Any five cards of the same suit, but not in sequence

Straight- Five cards in sequence, but not in the same suit

Three of a Kind- Three cards of the same value

Two Pairs- Two separate pairs

Pair- Two cards of the same value

Ginny's Brain to-do List

1. research colors for parts of brains
2. how to make brain stay on cardboard without sliding off (something stronger than superglue) * mrs. willis says try hot glue gun
3. type up list of brain parts

BAKER'S DOUGH RECIPE

3 1/2 cups flour

1 1/4 - 1 1/2 cup water

1 cup salt

Mix ingredients together in bowl. Knead until smooth.

Make shapes and bake at 300 degrees until set and

golden (1/2 hr to 1 hr).

GINNY,

THIS IS A VERY SIMPLE RECIPE FOR DOUGH. IT SHOULD WORK QUITE WELL FOR WHAT YOU HAVE IN MIND FOR YOUR BRAIN, ESPECIALLY FOR MOLDING.

Mrs. Willis

Horace D. Butts, D.S.W.
psychotherapist

99 Lorimer Street
Woodland Glen, PA

Ginny,
We will be meeting with the family therapist on Wednesday at 4:00. Please come straight home from school.
Mom and Bob

How do you feel about that?
the therapist asks
as we sit on his
palm tree covered sofa.
I mean, I know you have
to go to school for
a long time to be a
psychotherapist,
but all this guy learned
is how to ask
How do you feel about that?
he talks about the trouble
Henry gets into
and being sent away.
How do you feel about that?
And then he starts in
about Bob marrying Mom
and adjusting to a
new male presence.

How do you feel about that?
All I want to say is
Look,
    your name is Dr. Butts.
How do you feel about that?

BRAIN LOBES

PARIETAL LOBE – Controls perception of stimuli
(touch, pain, hot/cold)

TEMPORAL LOBE – Controls hearing and memory

OCCIPITAL LOBE – Controls vision

FRONTAL LOBE – Controls reasoning, emotions,
judgment, impulse control, spontaneity,
social behavior, motor activity, and speech

Mom,
I think Henry is missing
some of his frontal lobe.
That would explain a lot.
I'm sure Timmy
would be happy to donate
his.   Ginny

Bad Boy School of America

Knocking Sense Into Boys, Every Day

BY H. DAVIS

NO FUN HERE.

NO GARDEN GNOMES

OR TOILET PAPER

OR FIREWORKS.

NO GINNY TO SAY, "NO, HENRY!"

JUST RULES.

POLISH YOUR SHOES

MAKE YOUR BED.

I HATE PUSH-UPS

I THINK I REALLY SCREWED UP THIS TIME, GINNY.

beckysooboo1

INSTANT MESSAGE

Current Version: 1.1.0 (Build 1)
Latest Version: 2.5.0 (Build 23)

want 2 sleep over 2morrow night?

cancel   send

GinnyGirl

INSTANT MESSAGE

Current Version: 1.1.0 (Build 1)
Latest Version: 2.5.0 (Build 23)

that would be great!!

cancel   send

Dear Vamp

I would
it was unf
think you
Destroy Ev
Tell me wh

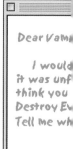

dumbwork

stinky poems

beckysooboo1

INSTANT MESSAGE

Current Version: 1.1.0 (Build 1)
Latest Version: 2.5.0 (Build 23)

cool!! I'll ask my mom 2 rent the new Vampire Vixens movie!!

cancel   send

nut'n

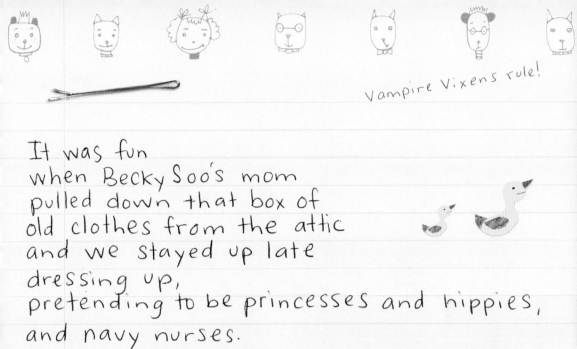

Vampire Vixens rule!

It was fun
when Becky Soo's mom
pulled down that box of
old clothes from the attic
and we stayed up late
dressing up,
pretending to be princesses and hippies,
and navy nurses.
Then her mom brought
in a plate of smores and
some hot cocoa
and we laughed so hard
I hiccupped.
But it wasn't until
the Vampire Vixens
beat the
evil mummy slugs
that things started
to feel normal.

A+
EXCELLENT JOB, GINNY!
YOU HAVE REAL TALENT.
MRS. WILLIS

Hoover

Ginny

Ginny's Brain to-do List

1. research colors for parts of brains
2. how to make brain stay on cardboard without sliding off (something stronger than superglue) * mrs. willis says try hot glue gun
3. type up list of brain parts

ʇɘƨuɟuoƆ ʏɒM ʇI móʜW oT

To Whom It May Confuse:

Supplies for Brain Project
1. flour + salt
2. paints -- acrylic
3. big piece of cardboard
   (to glue brain on)
4. hot glue gun + glue   do you really need this
5. Magic Markers   yes!!

SHARP
YOUR
SKILLS

I want to be a bee
and fly away
to a tree.
(That way I won't
have to learn
about stupid
triangles)

6.

.7 mm

PATIENT: Genevieve Davis

DIAGNOSIS:

Thirteen-year-old patient presents with a fractured right radius. Fracture sustained after falling from a tree when trying to climb up after her brother who was practicing his flying. Younger sibling is fine.

Ginny's NEW To-Do Goals

1. Survive seventh grade
2. Do a good job on brain project
3. Write to Henry once a week
4. Win Something. Anything
5. Maybe look into drawing lessons
6. Really ignore horoscopes!!!!!
7. ~~Go to the spring Fling~~ ?????>>>>>

Possible dates:

Becky Soo

Henry (if they let him out?)

Grampa Joe

~~Timmy~~

Bob (if I'm desperate)

LITATION CENTER   DAVIS, GENEVIEVE   Ident-A-Kid   Brace

LIFE SCIENCE -- LAB 8-3

PROBLEM: How do water animals react to stimuli?

PURPOSE: To observe how environmental changes affect the activity of brine shrimp.

MATERIALS:

1. microscope
2. droppers
3. salt + water
4. plastic bag
5. ice cube
6. cover slip
7. shrimp eggs
8. balance
9. graduated
10. rod
11. petri dish
12. foil

Judith   *gian* ☺   *mrs.*
willis   *Kimberly*   You should chave made them give you a yellow one!   *Becky Boo*

Bob   Want to go to the dumb dance?   I promise NOT to Fly anymore

Don't break any more bones! ★   - Brian Bukvic   ←

Louise   *Mom*   *Tammy*

David   *Tony*

Okay.
Ginny

CONCLUSION:

I personally think they are dead. They died because someone turned off the heater and it was really cold in here last night. Either that, or my lab partner killed them when he spilled that soda in the water. It's hard to say.

16. Fertilization is accomplished when:
   a) a pollen grain attaches to the stigma
   b) two sperm nuclei join
   c) a sperm nucleus joins with an egg nucleus
   d) pollen is moved from the stamen to the pistil

17. An advantage of sexual reproduction in angiosperms is that
   a) new plants may be formed, which are better adapted to survive in their environment
   b) plants with exceptional qualities desired by horticulturist may be produced again and again by vegetative propagation
   c) the spores of these plants may be distributed over a wider area
   d) monocots may be produced from dicots

18. The base of the flower is the:
   a) sepal   b) stem   c) receptacle   d) roots

19. The fluff on dandelion seeds is an adaptation for
   a) self-pollination   c) transfer of pollen
   b) photosynthesis   d) spreading the seeds

PART III - STUDY THE DIAGRAMS AND COMPLETE THE STATEMENTS

20 The transfer of cells from D to A is
   a) seed dispersal   c) fertilization
   b) vegetative propagation d) pollination

21 Union of sperm nucleus and egg nucleus takes place at
   a) A   b) B   a) C   d) D

22 After fertilization, structure E develops into the
   a) flower   b) pollen tube   c) tuber   d) fruit

23 The structure shown in diagram A is an enlarged
   a) ovary   b) root   c) tuber   d) stamen

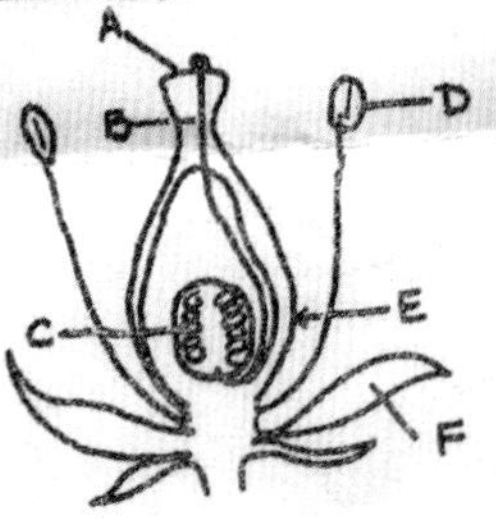

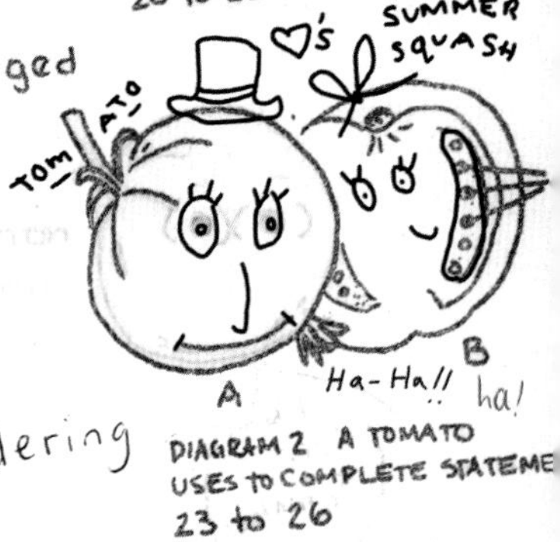

DIAGRAM 1 - A FLOWER
USES TO COMPLETE STATEMENT
20 to 22

DIAGRAM 2   A TOMATO
USES TO COMPLETE STATEMENT
23 to 26

what color's your dress?
   yellow. Why?
Because I have to buy you a corsage.
                    p.s. I am not wearing a suit

   I like daisies. In case you were wondering

hi

Have you ever noticed
how in movies the
the girl kisses the guy
as if there's nothing to it?
How come they never
Show the girl
leaning in,
eyes closed,
and then sneezing
so loudly
that the boy
jerks back,
bangs his head
on the wall,
and smacks his nose
on her ear?
I think it would be a
lot more realistic.
But I guess people
just don't want to see
those kinds of
movie moments.

(the second kiss was a lot better
although my ear still stings a little.)

Attention All

Household Members

Do not touch the brain in the basement!! (This means you, Timmy!!!)

Also, do not let Hoover in the basement! (This means you, Timmy!!!!)

Thank You,

Ginny ♡

After the year I've had I can safely say that middle school is worse than meatloaf. Only one more year to go, and it isn't looking much better. Becky Soo heard they're going to start serving "tuna fish surprise."

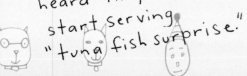

Dear Ginny,

I'm sorry to say that "the dog ate my homework," while a very amusing excuse, and not one I have heard very many times, does not substitute for the fact that you have not completed your quarter science project.

Sadly, I have no recourse but to give you an F.

Sincerely,
Miss Angelini

Attention Parental Units

I am hereby quitting school and resigning from being a daughter.

Sincerely,

Ginny

P.S. I am also moving to Vero Beach to live with Grampa Joe. He says it's fine with him.

Dear Miss Angelini,
Please accept this photo in lieu of Ginny's actual brain. As I'm sure you've heard, our dog ate her science project, and so this is the only proof we have of her hard work. We are all very proud of Ginny's brain.
Sincerely,
Bob Wright
(Ginny's stepdad)

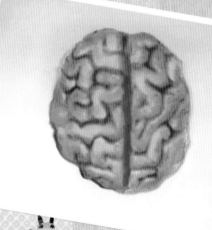

SUMMER ART WORKSHOP- Introductory Drawing

The class will meet three mornings a week, from 9:00 a.m.-12:00 p.m., in the art room of the middle school. Carpooling is recommended as there will be no buses.

SUPPLIES REQUIRED

1. SKETCHPAD (11" X 14")
2. CHARCOAL
3. PENCILS
4. INDIA INK AND PEN

I'M SO GLAD YOU'RE TAKING THIS CLASS!
MRS. WILLIS

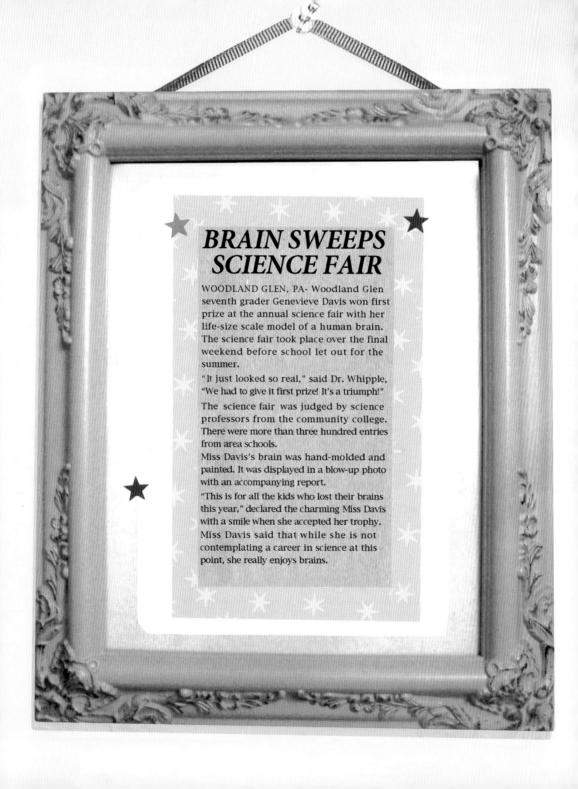

BRAIN SWEEPS SCIENCE FAIR

WOODLAND GLEN, PA- Woodland Glen seventh grader Genevieve Davis won first prize at the annual science fair with her life-size scale model of a human brain. The science fair took place over the final weekend before school let out for the summer.

"It just looked so real," said Dr. Whipple, "We had to give it first prize! It's a triumph!"

The science fair was judged by science professors from the community college. There were more than three hundred entries from area schools.

Miss Davis's brain was hand-molded and painted. It was displayed in a blow-up photo with an accompanying report.

"This is for all the kids who lost their brains this year," declared the charming Miss Davis with a smile when she accepted her trophy.

Miss Davis said that while she is not contemplating a career in science at this point, she really enjoys brains.

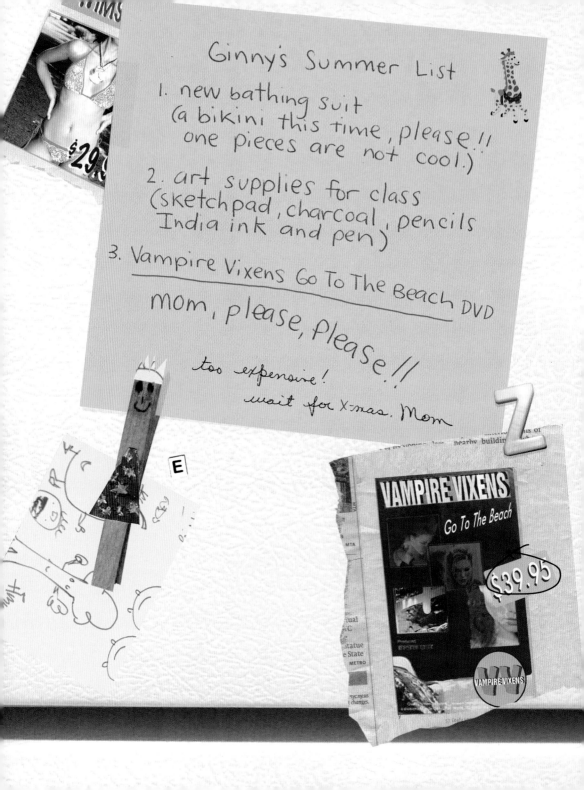

Ginny's Summer List

1. new bathing suit
   (a bikini this time, please!!
   one pieces are not cool.)

2. art supplies for class
   (sketchpad, charcoal, pencils
   India ink and pen)

3. Vampire Vixens Go To The Beach DVD

mom, please, Please!!

too expensive!

wait for X-mas. Mom

$29.9

E

VAMPIRE VIXENS
Go To The Beach
$39.95
VAMPIRE VIXENS

10 9 8 7 6 5 4 • The Library of Congress has catalogued the hardcover edition as follows: • Holm, Jennifer L. • Middle school is worse than meatloaf : a year told through stuff / by Jennifer L. Holm ; pictures by Elicia Castaldi. Summary: Ginny starts out with ten items on her to-do list for seventh grade, but notes, cartoons, and other "stuff" reveal what seems like a thousand things that go wrong between September and June, both at school and at home. • ISBN 978-0-689-85281-7 (hardcover) • [1. Middle schools—Juvenile fiction. 2. Middle school students—Juvenile fiction. 3. Middle schools—Fiction. 4. Schools—Fiction. 5. Family life—Fiction. 6. Remarriage—Fiction. • PZ7.H732226 Mid 2007 • [Fic]—dc22 • 2007298913 ISBN 978-1-4424-3663-3 (pbk) • ISBN 978-1-4424-3670-1 (eBook)

GREAT MIDDLE-GRADE FICTION FROM
Andrew Clements,
MASTER OF THE SCHOOL STORY

"Few contemporary writers portray the public school world better than Clements."—*New York Times Book Review*

Atheneum Books for
Young Readers

Published by
Simon & Schuster

KIDS.SimonandSchuster.com